ABNORMALLY

Abbey

ALLAN EVANS

Immortal Works LLC
1505 Glenrose Drive
Salt Lake City, Utah 84104
Tel: (385) 202-0116

© 2020 Allan Evans
www.evanswriter.com

Cover Art by Ashley Literski
http://strangedevotion.wixsite.com/strangedesigns

ISBN 978-1-953491-95-4 (Paperback)
ASIN B08GJJP7S8 (Kindle Edition)

This book is dedicated to my daughter, the real-life Abbey—and to all the ghosts that have haunted our home. Life has never been boring with all of you around.

1

HAUNTED HAPPENINGS

Shivering as the hairs stood on the back of my neck, I knew what I had to do. The stairwell was pitch dark, and of course nothing happened when I flipped the light switch. Nothing in my life goes that easy. If it did, I would definitely be someone else.

The basement was silent except for the sound of my own breathing. Still, I knew I wasn't alone. I hesitated for a moment, wondering if I was doing the right thing. "Should I Stay or Should I Go?" popped into my head and I couldn't help but smile.

My mom had instilled one important thing in me before she disappeared: an undying love of Eighties music—the single best decade for music. Wishing she were still here to share it with me, I slipped carefully down the wooden stairs, trying to be ninja.

The third step let out a slow creak as I eased my full weight onto it. The fourth step didn't do me any favors either, not that it made a difference. Someone—or something—was waiting for me.

A solitary figure stood at the base of the stairs. An old woman dressed in a flowing gown from a century ago beckoned me to proceed. A gust of wind kicked up—kind of strange, considering I was in a basement—and my hair swirled around my face. The woman's skin had a soft radiance that illuminated her in the dark, though her face remained shrouded in shadows. Her flesh was the color of a pale brown paper bag with faint shades of olive green, any trace of pink long forgotten. I could just make out the form of the ancient furnace hulking behind the old woman. The transparency of her drab, colorless clothing made it evident she was only partially here in our world.

Yeah, I see dead people.

If this woman wanted me down in the basement, she must have a reason. Let's have it then.

"Why are you here?" I asked. Stepping right up to the woman, the cold was so intense, I couldn't help but shiver. As close as I was, I still couldn't see her eyes. A veil of shadow covered her face, and I was left staring into a pit of darkness.

She didn't answer. Experience had taught me not to expect much —if anything—in the way of verbal interaction in these situations.

She ever so slowly raised her hand and reached for my cheek. It took everything I had to hold my ground.

A sensation of vertigo hit me as the woman's long-dead hand made contact with my skin. Angry faces and a violent struggle raced through my head, a chaotic whirl speeding by too fast to comprehend. I needed it to stop before I was swept away, unable to hold on to my own thoughts. It took every ounce of willpower to raise my hand. Drawing strength from my desperation, I focused on the spirit's hand and wrapped my fingers around the pale wrist. Making contact with her icy cold skin, I ripped the hand from my cheek.

The freight train of images careening through my head came to a screeching halt, and I started breathing again. This woman wanted me to know about her death, but there was nothing I could do. Clearly, she'd died ages ago.

Without warning, her hand came at me, shifting focus from my cheek to my throat. Her surprising strength brought me to my knees as I fought to keep the hand at a safe distance.

It was my own fault. I was the one who instigated this contact.

Lesson learned.

Twisting violently, I wrenched my hand from hers, and her power was lost as contact was broken. But not for a second did I believe the threat was over. I needed to end this.

"Time for you to leave. You're not wanted here. Go!" I shouted.

The breeze became a whirlwind and the overhead light blinked on, burning supernaturally bright. With a loud pop, the bulb shattered, leaving me covered in shards of glass and plunging me once again into darkness. The old woman was gone.

I hate dead people.

⸎

OPENING the door at the top of the stairs, I stepped into the light. Squinting, I made out a tall figure across the room, facing away from me. My eyes adjusted to the light, and I recognized my father standing at the kitchen sink, hands deep in the soapy water as he cleaned up our dinner dishes. "Hey, Abbey," he called over his shoulder. "What's going on in the basement?"

"Nothing," I answered. "I thought I heard something down there."

"I hope those squirrels haven't found their way back in. That's the trouble with these old houses."

Fighting back a smile, I reassured him. "No, Dad, not a squirrel to be found. Quiet as a graveyard down there."

I didn't like lying to my father, but some things were best left unsaid. He didn't need to know that my childhood ghostly experiences had continued with growing intensity—or that his daughter had become a certifiable spook magnet.

⸎

MY NAME IS ABBEY, and like most 14-year-old girls you meet, I'm relatively normal, at least until you get to know me. And then all bets are off.

As I'm sure you've picked up on by now, ghosts like me. Okay, "like" might be putting too much of a positive spin on it. They absolutely *are* attracted to me, though—like a fat kid is attracted to donuts.

There's a picture of me taken on my first birthday. I've got chocolate frosting smeared all over my smiling face, and my recently deceased great-grandmother looms behind me in the background. Guess she really didn't want to miss my party.

My mom told me a story about when I was young. She said I was sitting on the floor playing with my dolls and the door behind me had closed by itself. My mom had put down her book and opened the door. As soon as she was back on the couch, the door closed again. Frustrated, she got back up and placed a large book against the door to prop it open. The moment she was back sitting on the couch with her book open, the door slammed shut again. Mom was shocked to find the door locked and the book returned to its place on the bookshelf. This is how my life has always been; things have never been quite normal around me.

As I grew older, the ghosts kept coming. My mother got upset every time I told her about another dead visitor. She worried constantly. Sometimes she would cry, and I didn't like that at all. Eventually, I decided it would be better if I didn't tell her when a ghost made an appearance. I stopped telling my father most of the time, too. Maybe he still knew, but at least he had plausible deniability.

There's an art to keeping a straight face when a ghost walks into the room and you don't want the others around you to know. It takes supreme focus to keep talking to your mother about her day when a ghost passes through a closed door, glances your way and then does a double take. This one walked right up to me and began waving his hand right in front of my face—the same way you'd check to see if a person really could see through their super dark sunglasses.

There's a love-hate relationship happening where these ghosts are concerned. Sure, they intrude in on my life, coming at random times day and night and I've lost friendships when my abilities were discovered. I mean, I know it scares people, and really, who wants to hang out with the ghost girl?

But yet...

I don't know why, but I crave the ghostly contact. There's something about the feel of the chill running up my spine when I experience a ghostly appearance. I know it can be dangerous, but it's addictive, as well. I'm not sure what that says about me.

These days, I try to shelter my father as best as I can. Since it's just the two of us now, he already has a lot on his plate. I'll always be his little girl, and he'll always be the person I look up to most—which is exactly why my father's announcement changing my summer plans came as such a blow.

"No way. I have to spend the rest of vacation in River Falls? Wisconsin is the last place I want to finish out the summer. Why can't I come with you?"

My father gazed at me with tender eyes. I could tell it wasn't easy on him to leave me behind, either. "I really can't bring you this time. I'm going to a military base and there's not a place for children there. I did check, I really did."

My father, Constantine, was an investigative journalist who traveled the world writing books and magazine stories chronicling what he calls "the mysteries of our time." Whether it was psychic healers, UFOs, the Loch Ness Monster, Bigfoot, a government cover-up of an invisibility experiment gone horribly wrong, or off to Easter Island to examine the large stone heads, my father had been on some amazing journeys.

"Look, it's just six short weeks and then I'll be home and you'll start high school."

Arms folded, I held my ground. "That's the problem. You can't send me off to church camp the summer before high school. High school is important. I need to prepare."

A pained expression briefly colored his face. "I hate to disappoint you."

"Well, yeah. Adults have disappointed me all my life. Remember how much I liked Santa until I found out about all the amazing crap he gave my rich friends for Christmas." I couldn't help but giggle.

My father gave me a chuckle. "I also remember you got over it. And besides, it's not like it's really a camp," he said. "There are no leaky tents or run-down cabins. You'll be at River Falls College, living in the dorms. Camp Agape is the Cadillac of church camps."

"Camp Agape? Camps should have cool names like Camp Runamuck. Kathleen went to a camp last summer by a dried-up lake named Camp Lakebegone. *That* was a cool name."

"Okay, but a few weeks at church camp will be good for you," he said, giving me a look. "You may learn a thing or two." I narrowed my eyes at him, but he plowed on. "And besides, your mother would have wanted this for you."

Eyes down, I couldn't look at him. He wasn't playing fair. "I hate it when you play that card."

My father gave me a warm smile. "I know. It's my secret weapon. But, you'll have a summer vacation to remember for the rest of your life."

"That's exactly what I'm worried about," I called over my shoulder as I retreated to my room.

As it turned out, I was right to be worried.

2
WHERE IS THE LOVE?

One thing people learn about me—other than my teachers that is—is that I do my homework. I don't like going into situations unprepared. If I was going to be stuck at camp for the rest of the summer, I was at least going to be smart about it. Staying up way too late, I read as much as I could find about River Falls.

Roughly 30 miles from the Twin Cities, River Falls College is located along the beautiful Kinnickinnic River. The Kinni is well known in the area for its trout fishing. The town of River Falls has approximately 13,000 residents according to the last census and nearly 15 percent of that population was found to be living below the poverty line. According to pretty much anyone who has visited from the Twin Cities, River Falls is officially a small town.

"You'll be okay checking in by yourself?" my father asked as we got out of the car. I nodded, not sure what I should say.

"Sorry to just leave you at the curb, but I'm in danger of missing my flight."

The torrential downpour we encountered driving through the St. Croix Valley had put him behind his less-than-organized schedule. I'd been totally surprised when we were able to leave the house only twenty minutes behind that morning. Typically, every departure was delayed because my father would have to run back in the house for "just one more thing."

"At least the rain stopped; we managed to get ahead of it," he said, pulling the trunk release.

Three minutes later, after apologizing profusely for not escorting me inside, I was left alone with a stack of luggage as my father's taillights rounded the corner and disappeared for the next six weeks. *Heavy sigh.*

"Hey, Mom," I said out loud as I gathered my things. Not that she could hear me, but I found it helped when I talked to her. Don't judge. "Remember the Cyndi Lauper song we used to dance to? 'Girls Just Want to Have Fun.' Remember how we used to play it every time we made chocolate chip cookies? I'd be dancing around the kitchen waving the wooden spoons while you laughed until you couldn't stand up. Well, if you could see all the fun I'm having now, you'd be so jealous. But I better get inside. Talk soon."

Always a master of timing, the rain chose that moment to catch up and the downpour hit. Sometimes life is not at all fair.

With the rain coming down hard, the campus buildings were indistinct shapes, none of which looked particularly inviting. Almost on cue, a bell began to chime in the clock overlooking a nearby building. *Any port in the storm,* my father would say, and so I headed that way. Walking up the sidewalk, I paused to look at the clock, which continued its loud chiming.

Why would the clock chime now, when the time was 10:37?

This could be an odd place to spend my summer. I shook my head, sending raindrops flying and pushed through the massive wooden door.

Unsure which direction to go, I stood in the entrance, the rain pouring off me.

"Well, butter my butt and call me a biscuit. Y'all are looking mighty wet," a girl's voice said behind me, more than a hint of a southern accent in her voice. I jumped, startled by the proximity of the girl. I hadn't heard anyone approaching.

"Yeah, it's starting to look like rain out there," I replied, looking down at the small lake spreading out beneath me. Shivering, all I could do was laugh. "I'm the new girl, Abbey."

With a dramatic flair, she held out her hand. "Truly. As in truly, madly, deeply." Truly was a thin girl, standing several inches shorter than me, with pinned-up blonde hair and glasses. She wore an oversize powder blue sweater—though from the look of her, unless she bought her clothes from the children's department, almost everything would be oversized. "So sorry I have to run, but you'll find Mr. Johnson through those doors over there," she said, gesturing across the lobby.

"Thanks," I said turning back, but Truly was gone.

A group of teenagers, maybe twenty or so, sat on the floor staring at me. Some of them even had their mouths open. Hadn't they ever seen someone so wet, they were moments away from pneumonia? A grownup with his back to me loudly addressed the group. He paused, realizing there was a change in the room. It has been my experience adults don't like losing control of things, and so it wasn't a surprise when he turned around and fixed me with the sort of expression you might make when a particularly bad odor entered the room. The man was older, and had spiky brown hair with a bad dye job, as if he was trying to look younger than his AARP card might indicate.

I smiled at him, trying to look both sweet and vulnerable. He didn't appear to notice this, as his attention was instead focused on the puddle spreading beneath me onto the gym floor. Looking up at me, a cold fury clouded his face. This was not a man who radiated joy.

"And you are?" he asked as his greeting.

"Wet. And late. Sorry about the puddle," I said, looking down. "It's looking like rain."

Someone snickered from somewhere in the group. The adult in front of me was not amused, however. "Your name, please." At least I got the courtesy of a please.

"Abbey," I replied simply.

"Ahh, Miss Hill. Camp started yesterday, as you know."

"But I just found out yesterday I was coming here today." Great, I'm here for five minutes and I already feel like I'm behind.

"Nevertheless, you are still late. You'll have to wait to get settled in until we are through here. Why don't you have a seat." Not a question, he gestured to the side of the group. I dropped my bags where I stood and found a spot to sit by the edge of the group. The boy next to me gave me a wary look and slid away, putting some extra space between us.

"Camp Agape," I muttered to myself, shaking my head. "Where is the love?"

The boy next to me started coughing, though I suspected he was trying to cover his laugh. Mr. Johnson shot the boy a look, and then cleared his throat and spoke.

"Physical training is vitally important, as you'll need both a strong mind and a strong body to resist the temptations that come your way. Having the confidence to meet these challenges head-on will carry you through the battles to come. You are here," he said, looking around the room, "because you've lost these battles in the past. I'm here to tell you just because it has happened before doesn't mean it has to happen again. Work hard for the next six weeks and life will be different for you. You will be a new person, with a new attitude. You will have the strength to fight back from now on. Okay, Renata, you're first. Go climb the rope. And don't stop until you reach the top."

A skinny girl with dark hair got to her feet, nervously looked around the room and approached the rope. She paused at the bottom, gazing up the knotted rope to the ceiling twenty feet above. She looked less than confident as she paused before reaching for the thick rope with her small hands.

"It won't bite, Renata. Climb," he barked.

She jumped at the sound of his voice and surprisingly was halfway up the rope in a matter of moments.

"Okay," he said looking at us with a gleefully evil stare, "get into groups by the ropes. Everyone will need to climb the rope five times each." Groans echoed around the gymnasium. So far, this wasn't the church camp experience I'd been expecting. Maybe we'd be singing Kumbaya around the campfire later, but I was beginning to have my doubts. It wouldn't surprise me to learn this was the only camp on the planet without a campfire. This was an odd place.

3
THE SISTERS GRIMM

I was in serious pain. Climbing ropes wasn't as much fun as it looked—and it hadn't looked fun to begin with. My shoulders were sore, my thighs burned and my hands felt like I'd stuck them into a running garbage disposal. Forcing me to lug my suitcases all the way to my dorm in this condition likely constituted cruel and unusual punishment in some of the more enlightened countries around the world. In River Falls, however, you had to carry your burdens alone.

Moving at a speed a sloth would recognize and appreciate, I brought up the rear of the pack. The group as a whole looked tired and no one said a word as we made our way across campus. The rain had stopped, but the wetness lived on as I trudged through puddles, unable to lift my feet high enough to avoid soaking them.

We left the road and turned up a sidewalk heading toward an older brick four-story building. The structure looked neglected, giving me the mental picture of moldy mattresses and leaky faucets dripping endlessly. Of course, there would be dusty pictures of long-dead professors adorning the peeling wallpaper walls.

I can survive all this, I told myself. *I can do all things...*

I stopped dead in my tracks. "I can't do this," I said out loud, dropping my suitcases.

The plaque in front of the building read Grimm Hall. It was a sign if there ever was one. No way was I going to live in a building named Grimm Hall. Foreboding and bleak, this was not where I wanted to lay my head for the next six weeks.

"C'mon, I'll give you a hand with these," a welcoming voice

offered. Renata, the rope queen, stood next to me. "It's not as bad inside as it looks from out here. I've only counted four rats so far."

My head whipped around, and my jaw was open so wide a bear might consider my mouth a suitable location for hibernation. The twinkle in her eye clued me in that I'd been a victim of her charming sense of humor. I closed my mouth.

"Funny."

"Believe me, this isn't how I want to spend my summer vacation, either," Renata said, totally ignoring my comment. "I understand why you don't want to be here, I'm not much of a small town kind of girl, either. There's surprisingly little nightlife in River Falls. But you're stuck here just like the rest of us. You'll have to make the best of it."

Renata started up the sidewalk, carrying my suitcases with little difficulty. I assumed Renata expected me to follow her, as she never turned around, climbing the steps two at a time. "Walk with me," she called over her shoulder.

"Walk like an Egyptian," I said and couldn't help but giggle. Ahh, the Eighties had a song for everything. After doing my best Egyptian walk for a few delightful steps, I hurried to catch up to my suitcases.

"You don't want to take the elevator," Renata warned when we got inside. "They take forever and when they do show up, they make noises that, well, put it this way, don't inspire confidence. I prefer to be confident that when I step into an elevator, I will be able to walk back out of it."

The stairs had a musty smell but otherwise weren't too bad. My aversion to the stair climbers at the YMCA came back to haunt me once again, as I had to catch my breath on the second floor landing. After a moment, we continued up to the fourth floor where giant sheets of draped plastic blocked off the construction area.

"They're remodeling this middle section, so watch your step," Renata said as she pushed through the plastic. The hallway carpet had been pulled up; the room doors were removed and leaned against the walls as we made our way down the narrow corridor. Generally, there looked to be a lot of work still to be completed.

"I've heard there are quite a few buildings under construction on campus. This isn't as bad as some of the others," she added.

We came to another wall of plastic, and I was thankful we were going to be living in the remodeled section. As I held the sheet open for Renata and my suitcases, I realized my mistake. This was the old section, and they had yet to start work there. I had the peeling wallpaper part correct, but there weren't any photographs of long deceased professors on the wall. The walls were bare, with the occasional discolored rectangle spaced every few feet apart. Ahh, the pictures had been there but had been removed in anticipation of the upcoming remodel.

The doors had little signs cut into tent shapes taped to them, two on each door. The camper's names were written in Sharpie markers, all were girls.

At the end of the hall, we came to a door, and I found my name written on one of the construction paper tents. The name on the other read Stacia, apparently my roommate for the summer. I hoped she would be normal, but I wouldn't put any money on it. There hadn't been a normal minute since I got to camp.

Hoping for the best, I opened the door to find a small room with beds on opposite sides and a girl lying on her stomach on the far one. Stacia didn't appear to notice us, as I heard the music from her earbuds all the way across the room. Renata dropped the suitcases on the floor and said she'll catch up with me at lunch, leaving me alone with my new roommate.

I was torn, should I try to catch Stacia's attention or wait until she noticed me? I decided to unpack and wait until she saw me. It didn't take long to throw my jeans and T-shirts into the dresser drawers, and she still hadn't looked my way. I've always been impatient—so anyone who knows me wouldn't be surprised when a rolled up pair of socks slipped out of my hand and accidentally flew across the room, hitting Stacia.

In my defense, I absolutely hate being ignored.

Stacia pulled the buds from her ears, turning toward me—and I was stunned. It was Truly.

"Truly, what are you doing here? I thought my roommate was Stacia—at least that's what the sign on our door reads."

Sitting up, she said, "I get that a lot. Truly is my twin sister. We don't always get along, so we're in different rooms."

The southern accent was absent, but otherwise the two sisters were identical. "How come she has an accent and you don't?"

Smiling, Stacia nodded. "I get that question a lot, as well. Truly lives with our father in South Carolina, while I live with our mother in Minnesota. She claims to be the smarter of the two of us, but I like to think I'm the better looking one."

That seemed like a mighty thin hope to hang your hat on when you're an identical twin. But I wasn't going to be the one to burst her bubble. "Sorry about the socks, I can be a little clumsy sometimes." I shrugged.

Sitting up, she said, "I could see how it might happen. But I'm guessing you're not telling me the truth, either." Unsurprisingly, Stacia was just as petite as her sister. Most girls her size would fear a strong gust of wind, but Stacia radiated an intensity that would make the wind think twice about gusting in her direction.

Her eyes burned holes in me while she waited for my response.

I wasn't sure how to answer, as I couldn't tell if she was being serious or not. She looked grumpy with a side of psycho thrown in for good measure. I decided the truth was my best option.

"I *may* have tossed the socks to get your attention." I paused for effect. "I can be a badass that way."

Stacia nodded. "Don't even tell me how badass you are until you know how many Nutella packets I stole at hotel breakfasts in Florida over spring break." She held my gaze.

I'm not sure I've seen anyone blur the line between "not a morning person" and serial killer quite like my new roommate. But I nodded and said, "Yeah, I can totally see that." This appeared to make her happy, as Stacia gave me a great big grin.

"We'll have a great time hanging out this summer. Want to go explore?" she asked, changing topics abruptly. Stacia's smile promised more than a quiet walk around campus.

"How can I resist?" I asked as we headed for the door, eager to check out my new world.

4
TOUGH LOVING

B latantly ignoring the *Off Limits, Closed for Construction* and *Do Not Enter* signs, we entered the Crabtree Hall building through the front door. The smell of sawdust hit me right away, the scent triggering memories of my grandfather. He had a woodworking shop in his garage where he would spend hours building all sorts of things while hiding from Grandma. Whenever we visited, I would say a quick hi to her and then head for the garage to assist him in his woodworking.

Turning the corner, we headed down a hallway with no particular destination, just the desire to explore.

"Are your parents divorced?" Stacia asked randomly.

I wasn't sure how to answer the question, as my mom was no longer with my dad and me. But it wasn't because of divorce or death, and the story was still too painful to share. So, I took the easy route and simply answered, "No."

"You're lucky," she said. *But I didn't feel lucky.*

Stacia meandered as she talked, clearly more concerned with what she was saying, rather than where we were going. "Before they broke up, my parents used to argue all the time. I would pretend it was just a movie and I was playing the part of the girl who made them realize they still loved each other and put all the fighting behind them. But it never got better, even though I was sure they still loved each other."

"Love is a battlefield."

"Yes! That's so true." Stacia looked at me with such awe I had to come clean.

"I'll admit it; Eighties music is the soundtrack to my life. 'Love is a Battlefield' may have been an Eighties song by Pat Benatar, but it totally fits. I swear there's an Eighties song for every possible situation."

Stacia looked at me with a loopy grin. "Really?"

I nodded.

"Okay, then. What about when you're really happy?"

"Easy. 'Walking on Sunshine' by Katrina and the Waves."

Stacia nodded and continued. "What about when you're sad?"

"'Don't Stop Believin' by Journey."

Giggling, Stacia asked, "Let's say I woke up late, missed breakfast and I forgot to bring my lunch to the zoo field trip."

"'Hungry Like the Wolf' by Duran Duran."

More giggling. "You slip and somehow fall into the lion exhibit."

"'Do You Really Want to Hurt Me' by Culture Club."

"The mama lion looks at you like you're dinner. How do you save yourself?" Stacia asked, clearly enjoying herself.

"'I Ran' by A Flock of Seagulls. See? All of life is in Eighties music."

"Okay, I'm sold," Stacia said with a giggle.

Strident voices ahead broke up our music discussion and it became evident there was an argument in progress. We stopped outside an open door, staying close to the wall, not wanting to be discovered eavesdropping.

"I'm not going back up there. I'll work down here or over in Grimm, but that's all." The voice had an accent, Hispanic possibly.

"It's not up to you. I'm the site supervisor, so you go where I need you to go. Simple." This voice sounded older than the first one. It also had an annoyingly superior quality to it.

After a moment of hesitation, the first voice replied, "I...I can't."

"Are you afraid?" A mocking tone.

I was intrigued. Why was he afraid? I looked at Stacia and her eyebrow went up.

"It's not that I'm afraid, but things move by themselves. I'm on the floor, working on the trim and set down my hammer. It's right beside me. But when I reach for it, it's no longer there."

"So, you forgot where you set your hammer." The site supervisor wasn't exactly sympathetic.

"You don't get it," the voice sounded more agitated. "I'm still on my knees after using my hammer and now my hammer is across the room. On the counter. There's no way my hammer moved by itself from the floor to the counter. I was the only person in the room."

Stacia's mouth hung open.

The first voice continued. "I can't keep working here. Something's not right." The voice was getting louder as he headed for the door.

Crap, he was headed for us. Stacia and I looked at each other, panicked.

The second voice saved us. "Hold on, Juan. I'll have you start on the east wing." We didn't wait to hear what was said next, as we dashed down the hall, anxious to get away from the two men. Outside, we finally paused to catch our breath.

"That was close," Stacia said. "They almost found us."

I looked at Stacia. "Didn't you think his story was a bit strange? Hammers don't move by themselves."

"My mother always said superstition is the invention of an uneducated mind. The construction guy probably forgot he'd left his hammer on the counter." We walked back towards Grimm Hall, our exploration over for the time being.

I shook my head. "I don't know. I've seen some strange things, and this feels like one of those moments. I have to say, this is the oddest church camp I've ever visited."

It took a moment before I noticed Stacia was no longer walking alongside me. I glanced back to find her stopped in her tracks.

"Did you say church camp?" she asked with an odd look on her face.

"Yeah, my father said Camp Agape would be good for me. It's not how I wanted to spend my summer, though."

"Oh my," Stacia blurted and then began to laugh. You know how when someone keeps laughing and you can't help but join in? This wasn't one of those times.

"What?" I demanded. "What is it?" Though at this point, I wasn't so sure I wanted to know the answer.

Stacia caught her breath, wiping away a tear from the corner of her eye and officially ruined my summer.

"Camp Agape ended last week. This is Camp ToughLove."

"Camp *ToughLove?*"

Nodding, Stacia continued, her voice slow and measured, as though reading from a brochure. "Welcome to Camp ToughLove, the boot camp where troubled teens come to strengthen their mind, body and spirit in a highly disciplined arena." She rested a hand on my shoulder, which I took to be a gesture of sympathy. "And the emphasis here is squarely on discipline. This will not be a pleasant summer vacation at church camp."

5

BUNKIN' WITH A
HORSE RUSTLER

I was absolutely numb: a *Bachelor* candidate, totally brain-dead sort of numb.

Lying on my bed staring at the ceiling, I tried to make sense of my predicament. How could this have happened? My father wouldn't have knowingly sent me to a boot camp, would he? It wasn't like I'd ever been a troubled teen. Sure, I didn't like to clean my room, and he always had to remind me to put away my dinner dishes, and I watch some cable shows I wasn't supposed to watch. And—oh my God, I *was* a troubled teen!

My mind raced as I stole a glance toward Stacia. What was she in for? Was I going to be sharing a room with a murderer, a car thief or a drug dealer? No, none of those felt right. She was too sweet. It had to be something smaller—maybe she was in for fighting with her sister, stealing her neighbor's Sunday newspaper or horse rustling. Either way, I wasn't going to sleep with my back to her; it never hurt for a girl to be too careful.

I had zero idea what I was up against being in a boot camp. If it were a church camp, we'd be playing games, singing songs, and studying bible verses. Maybe not how I'd prefer to spend my summer, but I could handle it. Here at Camp ToughLove, I had my doubts we'd be singing songs at all. Instead, the warden would probably have us out in a field somewhere, digging holes in the hot sun.

I sat up abruptly and announced, "I hate digging holes."

The look I got was priceless. No doubt Stacia was now the one with serious concerns about the stability of her roommate. "Huh?" she asked eloquently.

"Holes," I explained. "I don't want to spend my last summer before high school digging holes for the sinister lady warden. I like the idea of getting a tan, but it'll totally destroy my nails."

Stacia was once again laughing uncontrollably—again at my expense. I'm glad I could be a comfort to my horse-rustling roommate. "You're too funny," she said. "There's no warden, no holes and no criminals. The kids are here because of issues they've had. Maybe they've suffered from depression, chemical abuse or have trouble relating to others. Parents send their kids here to better prepare them to face life's challenges. It's tough, but you'll survive," she said with a smile.

Okay, I could handle this. No digging. No holes. No lady warden with rattlesnake venom in her fingernail polish. "So, what do we do here then?"

Stacia smiled broadly. "Did you ever see one of those movies where somebody joins the army and they have to survive basic training? It's like that. There will be rope climbing, pushups, two mile runs, still more pushups and the occasional obstacle course. Other than physical training, we get classwork in science and English, and there is also a holdover from Camp Agape: a bible study. Mind, body and spirit, we get it all."

While I processed this new information, Stacia continued, "There will always be someone telling you what to do, when to do it, and how to do it—and you've got to do it. It probably won't kill you."

Five minutes later, I was outside on my cell phone calling my father. There was no way I was staying. It was clearly a mistake I ended up at this camp. The important thing to remember is my father talked about Camp Agape, not Camp ToughLove. His intention was I'd spend my summer there, learning about religion and things—not in a boot camp with troubled teens. Infuriatingly, the call went right to his voice mail.

"Dad, it's me," I said, trying to sound as worried as possible. "There's been a mistake, a colossal mistake. Camp Agape ended last week and now I am trapped in a boot camp for wayward youth.

Please call me back before I'm transformed into a bloodthirsty marine or murdered in my sleep by a troubled teen suffering from relationship issues. Please call soon."

Hanging up, I realized there was another way to fix this. The camp administration was set up at the University Center, one of the more modern buildings on campus. I headed there, confident my outrage at being enrolled at the wrong camp would elicit sympathy.

It wasn't the first time I've been wrong.

"You've got to be kidding me," the sour-faced man said. "You've been left at the wrong camp? And I'm supposed to take your word for it? You wouldn't be the first to try to get out of the camp because it's too tough." He gave a dramatic pause before continuing. "In fact, I've been expecting someone to try to talk their way out of here." He opted not to steeple his fingers while saying this. What a wasted opportunity.

"I have your online registration right here," he said, pointing to his laptop screen. "Constantine Hill registered you on Monday for this camp. Since our church camp ended last week, he should have noticed it when he completed the registration form. The only way to leave camp early is to have your father stop by—and then, I can only release you to him. However, there are no refunds after camp has started."

I looked at his eyes, willing him to believe me, so he would help me escape this tragic mistake. "Please, I can't reach him. He's away on business and can't answer his phone. I know he'd want me to be happy and not here, suffering in the wrong camp." I tried to give him my best puppy-dog look.

He wasn't budging. At all. "Our camp is named Camp ToughLove for a reason, Miss Hill. Parents want what is best for their children, even if it means enduring short-term hardship to create a better, stronger child in the long run." He gave me what might pass for a smile in some shabby traveling carnival. "There is a bright side. A summer here will keep you out of juvenile detention in the future."

Some bright side. As I walked back to my room, defeated, I

started talking to my mom again. "Hey, Mom. Hope you're doing okay wherever you are. Life here at camp has taken a turn for the worst. But I'll hold on. I mean I'm 'Livin' On A Prayer,' but if Bon Jovi thought you could make it with just love to get you through, then it's good enough for me."

I hope Mr. Bon Jovi knew what he was talking about.

6
THE MALE OF THE SPECIES

Two figures shimmered in the twilight. The day's last rays of light shined through the hallway windows, illuminating their transparent nature. Their bodies had no mass, simple shadows playing tricks with the light. These were spirits. Walking steadily in their direction, I was drawn to them. They had their backs to me, heads leaning in conspiratorially, having a conversation only they could hear.

I stepped up, curious to know what they were discussing. There are times when my curiosity has gotten me into trouble. This was one of those times.

It was sudden, it was vicious and there was nothing I could do about it. A hood was thrown over my head, cutting off all light and air. My hands beat without effect against the heavily corded muscles holding the hood in place. I was frantic, knowing I could die right there in the hallway.

Without any reason, my mom's face popped into my head and I was able to force out a semblance of calm. I stopped struggling, letting my arms slide off my attackers and after a moment, allowed my knees to give out. I wanted my attacker to relax—let his guard down however briefly—so I could gain some advantage.

With my attacker now forced to hold me up, I put all my weight on my right foot while I kicked back as hard as I could with my left. I wanted to wallop this guy and I might have, but I missed, not connecting with anyone. Thrown off balance, I pitched to the floor. Clawing to get the hood off, my screams echoed down the hallway as I realized there was no hood.

My gasps were the only sound as my heaving lungs fought to replenish oxygen. Face planted into the gross carpet—some twenty years past its freshness date—left me sick to my stomach. The post-adrenaline shakes took me and I wanted to puke.

I rolled over and there was no sign of an attacker or the pair of ghostly visitors. It was only me.

What just happened?

I wished I knew.

Usually, these paranormal experiences were sudden and powerful, and then *wham-bam*-gone, but this one had left me fearing for my safety. There was something about this place that had dialed up my spookometer so far past normal, I couldn't even see normal anymore.

I looked over my shoulder as I hurried down the hallway, anxious to be with other people—even if it was the troubled teens of Camp ToughLove.

ᗺᗺ

MOVING AS A GROUP, we headed to the University Center for gathering time after dinner. I shuffled along with Stacia, bringing up the rear.

While not exactly an exciting meal, the Sloppy Joes and greasy potato chips had filled me up. What I found most interesting during dinner was watching the interpersonal dynamics of the other residents. Given the Camp ToughLove camper's supposed inability to cope with conflict and relationships, I thought it would be interesting to observe their behaviors. I began to feel like Jane Goodall as she observed the chimpanzees with nothing more than a notebook and a pair of binoculars.

I noticed the boys' quest to be recognized as the dominant male. The posturing, the swagger, the glaring eyes. It wasn't long before I witnessed actual physical contact as a pair of large males crossed paths and bumped shoulders. Out here in the wild, there were no manners, no halfhearted mumblings of "excuse me." Both males continued on their chosen path, acting oblivious to the offered challenge. To react would be to show weakness. I saw none.

The females have their own social rituals. They tend to group in pods, where they scrutinize not only the stray individual females, but also members of rival pods. I began to notice the most vocal females—the ones loudly expressing their derision of other females—have the largest pods surrounding them. The correlation played itself out again and again throughout our dinner hour. My hypothesis—which I intended to prove during my forced stay here—was that the less dominant females would group into these pods as they offered protection from the most scathing of female leaders.

The most feared female at Camp ToughLove was Carrie. Although her stature was small, her razor-sharp wit could bring the strongest to their knees. It was almost funny, the juxtaposition between her sweet smile and the words that came out of her mouth. I would have to make every effort to avoid being on the receiving end of her fury. It may be difficult to believe, but I could keep a low profile. That's why I brought up the rear as we entered the University Center.

Our group spread out while Stacia and I continued to the Kinnickinnic River Theater. The large auditorium was where we held our evening gatherings. No singing around the fire at this camp.

As we entered the empty theater from the back and made our way down to the front, Stacia stopped and grabbed my arm. "Do you see that?" Her voice had an odd quality to it. Fear will do that to a person.

I looked in the direction of her gaze. The two seats on the aisle in the front row were rocking. By themselves. No other seats were moving. I glanced at Stacia, whose raised eyebrows and wide eyes told me a lot about her state of mind. She was terrified.

I had no explanation for what I was witnessing. However, I don't have explanations for most of the things that happened to me. Some things just have to be accepted. "Come on," I said grabbing her hand and dragging her down the aisle.

We moved deliberately toward the rocking seats as they continued to move, back and forth, back and forth. As we got closer, the rocking slowed and stopped altogether. Stacia peered around my shoulder staring at the seats, no doubt looking for a conventional explanation for the movement. But, there wasn't anyone hidden there. No wires were attached and no drafts of air to make the seats rock by themselves. At the moment, the seats were deathly still, with not a sign of the animation we'd witnessed moments before.

"I think we should sit here," I said as I gestured to the offending seats.

"Are you out of your mind?" Stacia asked with a hint of hysteria creeping into her voice.

"You'll be fine," I said as I pulled her down beside me. Stacia white-knuckled both of her armrests as though she was preparing to be launched on the *Steel Venom* roller coaster at Valley Fair. "Nothing can hurt you here," I reassured her, speaking in the most calming tones I could muster. "We are safe."

It took a few long moments before I heard Stacia let out the breath she'd been holding. Her eyes darted around the room and, apparently not spotting any immediate threats, her fingers relaxed, the color returning. Stacia's breathing evened out as the others took their seats, the danger over.

Stacia was going to have to get used to this sort of thing if she planned on hanging out with me. Abnormally Abbey was in the house.

7
HOOKED ON GHOST STORIES

After our evening gathering—really a thinly disguised lecture on personal responsibility by one of the counselors—we moved outside. The lecture wasn't at all relevant to me, however, as I was the responsible one in our family—I looked out for both my father and myself. The talk was given by Ms. Neuman, an exotic-looking woman dressed completely in black. She held the interest of the group, especially the boys—they followed her every move as she strode around the stage in her way-too-fashionable-for-camp heels. She said we needed to admit we're responsible for the way we think and feel, not other people or events. It is our life, and we are in charge of it.

Well, duh.

As it turned out, I was wrong; our camp actually had a campfire. It was at Glenn Park, right across the Kinni River. The interesting part was how we had to cross the river. The old-fashioned rope and plank bridge swayed and bounced with every step. The motion in the pit of my stomach was not a feeling I enjoyed. But I kept my eye on the girl in front of me and was across before I knew it.

The night was warm and the mosquitoes hadn't found us yet. The counselors directed us to sit on one of the twelve ginormous tree stumps encircling the campfire like a large clock face. I found myself sharing one with Stacia and a girl named Brooke. Brooke had short blonde hair and vacant eyes. I hadn't seen her say a single word to anyone. Was she just shy and reclusive, or possibly more of an angry loner? Who could tell when she wouldn't say anything?

Stacia and I shared a glance as we listened to several girls talking.

"I've heard this place is haunted."

My head whipped around. *Haunted?* Someone was speaking my language. Two girls were huddled together, whispering.

"Yeah," one said. "Some of the girls have heard things. Voices, phantom basketball games, animals even."

"That doesn't surprise me. There is a slaughterhouse on campus, you know."

"No way."

"Way. River Falls is big into agriculture."

"Still weird, if you ask me."

"It gets weirder, though. One of the custodians told me there used to be an empty house on campus. Apparently, homeless people were living in the attic. Somehow the building caught on fire and they were all trapped as the building burned to the ground, leaving them to die a horrible death."

"Tragic."

"I know. But, there's more. The custodian said there was a pool on campus paved over after a student drowned."

"That sounds like a rather extreme reaction."

"I know, right? I guess the circumstances were rather bizarre. The girl's roommate told school officials the drowned girl was hearing voices."

"Voices? Never a good thing."

"So true. The voices were getting increasingly insistent, demanding she swim with them. Alone. At night."

"And she went? Epic."

"I know. There's still more."

"More? This place is giving me the shivers." I knew the feeling as my own arm was covered with goosebumps.

"A teacher hung himself just a few years ago."

"That stuff happens, right? It's unusual, but not really paranormal."

"This is. The custodian swears he was there and saw it."

"Saw what?"

"The body. It was swinging, as it hung from a rope tied to an exposed beam in a faculty house."

"So?"

"Don't you get it? They found the teacher's hanging body—some twelve hours after the deed was done—and the body continued to swing. The custodian said the campus police officer put his hand on the teacher, stopping the motion. However, the second he let go, the swinging started again. The campus police officer ran, leaving the custodian there by himself. The body swayed unrelentingly until the River Falls fire department cut it down. Two hours later."

"Epic. Truly epic." The girls fell silent, lost in their thoughts. Stacia and I glanced at each other. I could only guess what she was thinking. We held onto an uncomfortable silence waiting for something to happen.

It didn't take long. Like most campfires I've had the pleasure to sit around, there was an undeniable pleasure listening to scary stories in the light of a fire. With no idea of what lies waiting in the surrounding darkness, yet in the comfort of the fire, you enjoy hearing tales that make you squirm.

A girl was sharing a story, telling us about a ghostly killer who was stalking teenagers, on a night just like this, in a camp just like this. When...

One of the boys jumped up behind us with a ghastly shriek.

Some of the girls screamed. Several of the boys fell right off their stumps, and the rest of the group started laughing when they realized the prank.

As everyone settled down, Corey said, "I have one."

The group turned in his direction as he stood up. "The reports had been on the radio all day, though she hadn't paid much attention to them. It seemed people were always escaping from jail. The report said a crazy man had escaped from the state asylum. They were calling him the Hook Man since he had lost his right hand and had it replaced with a hook. He was a killer, and everyone in the area was warned to keep watch and report anything suspicious. But this didn't interest her. She was more worried about what to wear on her date."

Corey prowled around the campfire as he told his story. "After trying on several different outfits, she was finally ready and went outside to meet her boyfriend who had been waiting on the porch. After the drive-in movie, they found a secluded spot at the local lover's lane. She cuddled close to her boyfriend as they kissed to the sound of romantic music on the radio.

"Then, the announcer came on and repeated the warning she'd heard earlier. An insane killer with a hook in place of his right hand was loose in the area. Suddenly, the dark and moonless night didn't feel so romantic to her. The lover's lane was well off the beaten path and the perfect spot for a deranged madman to lurk." Corey said this directly to a pair of girls who shivered noticeably.

Moving on, Corey continued. "Worried, the girl said 'Maybe we should get out of here,' pushing her boyfriend away. 'That Hook Man sounds dangerous.'

"'Aw, c'mon babe, it's nothing,' her boyfriend said, trying to get in another kiss. She pushed him away again.

"'No, really. We're all alone out here. I'm scared,' the girl said." Corey's impression of the girl's voice was comical.

He continued. "They argued for a moment. Then the car shook a bit as if something...or someone...had touched it. She shrieked and said, "Get us out of here!"

Corey walked in our direction.

"'Jeez,' her boyfriend complained in disgust, but he turned the key and went roaring out of the lover's lane screeching his tires. They drove home in stony silence, and when they pulled into her driveway, he refused to help her out of the car. He was being so unreasonable, the girl fumed to herself while opening her door and stepping out into the driveway. Whirling around, she slammed the door as hard as she could. And then she screamed."

Corey was a large boy and his shadow threw much of our stump into darkness. He looked right at us as he spoke rapidly. "Her boyfriend leaped out of the car and caught her in his arms. 'What is it? What's wrong?' he shouted. Then he saw it. A bloody hook hung from the handle of the passenger-side door."

Several of the girls gasped as Corey let out a maniacal-type laugh and we applauded his performance. "Who's next?" he asked.

Everyone looked around and Stacia elbowed me. "Abbey has one." She nodded at me.

I'm guessing she wanted me to tell the story of what we heard with the construction workers, but with a counselor here, I didn't want to incriminate myself by saying I overheard it in an off-limits campus building.

"Okay," I began. "This happened in a little town in Ireland. It was a moonless night as the mother of all rainstorms had set in, and Paul was hitchhiking on the roadside. The poor guy was not able to see beyond a foot due to the strong storm. Suddenly, he heard a car coming towards him. The car came into view and stopped close by. Wanting to get out of the terrible storm, Paul got into the car without thinking. He sat for a moment, catching his breath and looked around. Oh my God! There was nobody behind the wheel!"

I stood up, talking louder. "The car began to move. Paul looked at the road and noticed a curve coming his way. Petrified, and still in shock, Paul began to pray for his life. But, just before the car hit the curve, a hand appeared through a window and moved the steering wheel. Paul was almost paralyzed in terror as the ride went on, watching as the hand suddenly appeared every time the car approached a curve. At last, he somehow managed to open the door and jumped out of the horrible car. Without even looking back, he ran to the nearest town through the storm. When he reached the town, he was completely wet, exhausted and not able to utter a single word due to his state of shock. Paul was very shaken and went to a nearby bar, asking for two shots of Scotch."

I started meandering around the circle of stumps. "Still frightened and trembling, Paul told everyone in the bar about his horrifying experience. When he spoke about the spooky car without a driver and the mystical hand appearing out of nowhere, everyone was frightened, realizing the guy was telling the truth."

As I got to the top of the circle by the counselor, I stopped and turned to face the group. Trying not to smile, I continued. "After half an hour, two guys entered the same bar. One said to the other, 'Hey, there's the guy who jumped into the car while we were pushing it.'"

My punch line was met with several groans. Thankful for any reaction, I found my seat next to Stacia. "Good one," she told me.

"Time for bed," the counselor called out. "Let's go." There was a general grumbling, but we got up and headed for the dubious comfort of Grimm Hall.

Taking up our customary position at the back of the group, Stacia elbowed me again. "Why didn't you tell them about the construction worker losing his hammer?"

"Why didn't you?" I threw it back at her.

"Too shy," she said with a smirk. "Hey, do you believe in ghosts?"

I looked at her for a long moment. "Yes, I do. I've seen one or two."

Stacia looked surprised. "Really?"

I nodded. "Really. When I was little, one of my earliest memories was sitting on the couch, coloring next to my mother. I remember asking, 'Who is that?' My mom looked around, not seeing anyone. She thought I was kidding and asked who I saw. I told her, 'I see an old woman in the window. She has glasses and a funny white shirt where the collar goes way up on her neck.' My mom couldn't see the woman, but she said it sounded like my deceased great grandmother. I could see her plain as day, reflected in the window."

"Whoa," Stacia said. "Have you seen anything like that since?"

I paused, unsure how best to respond. "I see a lot of things," I replied, trying to be enigmatic. As a teenager, it goes against my nature to say or do anything to set me apart from everyone else.

"But you've seen ghosts since you were a child?" Stacia asked.

I nodded. "On occasion. But I've simply learned, more or less, to accept these experiences as a part of my life."

We took the steps at the front entrance to Grimm Hall. The group dissolved as we headed for our rooms, leaving me and Stacia alone. "You *are* a little unusual, aren't you?" Stacia said with a grin.

She didn't know the half of it. I'm like a real life "Thriller" video. There's things lurking in the dark and as you close your eyes and hope it's just your imagination. Grisly ghouls wait behind every tree.

Grrr.

8

A NICE MORNING FOR THE RUNS

What a brutal morning.

A certified night owl, I wasn't much of a morning person, and I was startled awake by what I believed to be a frying pan hammering on our door. With just enough time to throw on some shorts, a T-shirt and a pair of running shoes, Stacia and I were forced into the dim light of dawn to run for our lives.

It may not have been that extreme, but Mr. Johnson was yelling at us. Stacia and I fell to the back of the bunch, as I gasped for air. Mr. Johnson loudly condemned us for our apparent lack of effort, even though I was trying. He may be used to being awake this early in the morning—when only the over-achieving birds are up getting their disgusting breakfast—but my body was rebelling. My mind wasn't awake enough to give my muscles direction, so my sleep-deprived body was left to flail on its own. Not a pretty sight, my gait was slow and awkward, but I tried my best and kept putting one foot in front of the other.

There was a point in the run that took us along the edge of the woods overlooking the river. This was the section where our group got spread out and I found I was all alone. Stacia had given up her attempt to help me stay with the group, but I managed to hold onto a slow and steady pace.

This was also the part that got strange.

I realized I was near the woods, but the sounds were unusually loud. At first, it was the crickets. The volume swelled as nearly every insect within a quarter of a mile joined in. The birds started up too, giving a near constant background of chirping. To add to the swelling nature choir, larger-sounding birds began to squawk intermittently.

My field of vision narrowed as the surrealistic nature of this experience heightened. The sheer noise of the event was unnerving. An unexpectedly close shriek brought home the fact these weren't Wisconsin birds. My gut—as well as my ears—told me I was experiencing some sort of paranormal sensory shift. I'd been transported far, far from River Falls.

Just as I was expecting a jungle cat to step out, eyeing me up as a potential between meal snack, the experience came to an end. The noise level dropped from a turn-your-music-down-before-I-call-the-cops to a volume more suited for a doctor's waiting room. I looked around to see if anyone else heard it, but there wasn't anyone in sight. I shook my head at the mystery and continued running.

As I'd guessed, I was the last to finish.

Mr. Johnson, who was rapidly becoming my least favorite person, stood with his arms folded across his chest.

Looking at his face, I got the feeling he wasn't happy with me.

"Miss Hill needs a bit more conditioning as it turns out. And since she can't run by herself, the lot of you need to join her. One more time gang, same course, but faster this time. Now go!" he barked.

And after he threw me under the bus, it didn't take long for the rest of the group to join him. I got some shoves and a few threats hissed at me as the group swarmed past. *This was so unfair*. Still standing in place, I caught my breath, feeling the ache as each and every muscle in my legs complained in their own special way.

Mr. Johnson stepped into my space and leaned close. "Miss Hill, you do not want to be last again. Go," he said with a menacing undercurrent in his tone.

I wasn't going to stay and argue with him, as much as he needed to be put into his place. Staying at the rear of the pack, I came to a realization. This camp wasn't for me and I would do whatever it took to get out of there.

I MANAGED to finish the run in the middle of the pack. As we headed down the final stretch, four of the group slowed down greatly, allowing me to get into the middle. I felt a hand on my low back nudging me forward. But, I don't believe for a second it was out of kindness, as self-preservation ruled the day at camp. If I had to guess, I would say several of the smarter kids wanted me to stay out of last place so they wouldn't have to repeat the run yet again.

Walking to the University Center, I tried calling my father again. Of course, it went directly to voicemail.

"It's me, Dad, still stuck at the prison camp. Please call as soon as you get this message. It's worse than you might think here. I heard about an escaped killer almost catching this poor girl. Please call me before it happens again." Okay, I knew I took things out of context, but they do it all the time on the news programs my father watched. And if there was one thing I was good at, it was picking up on adult behaviors.

While I was on the second leg of my run, my oxygen-starved brain came up with a pretty good idea. If I couldn't get my father's help, I was going to need the help of another adult to escape my unjust incarceration. And I knew just the person.

I remembered seeing an advertisement for an attorney on the dog-eared copy of the yellow pages I saw on the information counter. I steered clear of the grumpy man who gave me absolutely no help yesterday. He was talking to another adult, no doubt they're discussing how they could be meaner to more kids. I simply walked around the back side of the counter, grabbed the phone book and headed over to the seating area.

Right on the cover, among all the ambulance-chasing attorneys, was the smiling face I remembered: Brian A. Thompson, Attorney-at-Law. "I'm here to help you." Nice and simple, no personal injury horror stories or promises of million dollar settlements. Just an offer to help.

I decided right then and there, I wanted Brian Thompson, Attorney-at-Law, on my side. I dialed his number.

"Brian Thompson." He answered right way and his voice sounded friendly enough.

"Mr. Thompson," I said trying to sound older than my years. "I need your help."

"I'm here to help you," he said, echoing his phone book advertisement. It made me feel warm as I pictured his smile.

"What is the nature of your problem?"

"There's been a tragic mistake and I'm being held against my will."

"So you're being incarcerated?" He clearly had a sharp legal mind and I knew I'd be sprung free in no time. "Are you in the Pierce or St. Croix County lockup?" he asked.

"Actually, neither. I'm being held at the River Falls campus."

"Ahhh," Brian Thompson dragged out the word as he processed this left turn I'd thrown at him.

"I'm at the boot camp here, Camp ToughLove. It was a big mistake. My father thought he was signing me up for a church camp —the church camp that ended last week. And now the staff here won't let me leave."

There was a palpable hesitation coming out loud and clear through the phone. Don't let me down, Brian Thompson, Attorney-at-Law.

"Can I ask how old you are, Miss...?"

"Hill. I'm Abbey Hill. And I'll be fifteen on my next birthday."

More hesitation. "Where are your parents? If it was your father's mistake, he should be able to help you."

My turn to hesitate. "I can't reach him. He's at a super-secret military base, researching for a book. I've been leaving messages on his cell phone, but so far he hasn't called back."

"I see. How about your mother then?"

"She disappeared. She went to Venezuela for work and just never came back." I didn't want to talk about my mother with this stranger.

My mother, Katherine, worked with the Doctors Without Borders organization, caring for the sick on basically what were extended mission trips. She went to troubled locations where civil wars and fighting occurred and though the doctors wouldn't take sides in armed conflicts, they were honor-bound to alert the public of abuses occurring beyond the headlines. Such candor had been known to raise ill will toward the doctors, often putting them further in harm's way. And though I could never accompany her, I was proud of her work and enjoyed the stories my mother would tell me upon her return.

It happened when I was 11. My mother left for a trip to South America and disappeared. There was a massive search by the State Department, covering much of Venezuela, where she was last heard from. However, she had completely vanished—not leaving a single clue as to her whereabouts. My father flew down to conduct his own search after the State Department gave up. He returned empty handed and completely devastated. Life was never the same for us after that, as we both struggled greatly with her absence. A girl should not have to grow up without her mother.

"I see," he said again as I felt all hope fading away. "I don't suppose you have any relatives you can call on, do you?"

I was shaking my head, which was so stupid because I was on the phone. This had been a bad idea. Then the first bit of luck I'd had all week came out of nowhere.

"Miss Hill, why don't I meet with you in person? I could be there around lunchtime. There's a possibility I could do something to help. Let's meet and see what happens."

We made arrangements for my savior, Brian Thompson, Attorney-at-Law, to find me later. Maybe I was going to get out of Camp ToughLove after all.

9
BOW CHICKA WOW WOW

Lunchtime at camp was like being back in elementary school. You got in line and waited, holding the still damp plastic tray. Even though you're hungry, you're not sure you want to eat the mystery meat or tuna surprise. But, since I skipped breakfast to make my call, I was going to eat it—even if it was so gross, I had to close my eyes. So I waited in the back of the line for my turn.

But then...

I smelled the scent of a boy.

I hadn't even noticed someone stepping in front of me to grab an apple, as I was so engrossed in my food options. His intoxicating fragrance pulled all thoughts away from food. My eyes took a stroll over the tall figure standing inches away. His damp dark hair, freshly showered, was worn long. A white T-shirt—snug in all the right places—showed off his broad shoulders, and his ripped jeans held my attention longer than they should. He turned, forcing my gaze up.

"Sorry to butt in," he said with a dazzling smile and stepped out of line with banana and apple in hand. "I'm Turner. And you are...?"

"Abbey."

"Nice to meet you," he said. I followed his every step as he gracefully maneuvered through the crowd to his table. He must be new as I would have remembered someone so...memorable.

Bow chicka wow wow.

A tall man waved at me from across the room. Brian Thompson was here. Carrying my lunch tray, I crossed the room to meet with my new attorney. With a last glance in the new boy's direction, I almost walked into a trashcan, not exactly the impression I wanted to make.

With as much grace as I could muster, I sidestepped the obstacle and joined my attorney, Brian Thompson.

Dressed casually, wearing a tweed sport coat with elbow patches and khakis, Mr. Thompson had gray-flecked chestnut-colored hair. His rather pleasant face reminded me of a friendly uncle. He pulled a notebook from his worn leather briefcase, reaching across the table to shake my hand. "A pleasure to meet you, Miss Hill."

Still feeling rather flustered by the new boy, I forced myself to focus as I shook my attorney's hand. "You too, Mr. Thompson."

Brian Thompson gave me a serious yet compassionate look he must have used to great effect in the courtroom. "I am here to help you."

No wonder the phrase was in his advertisement; he said it all the time. Getting directly to the point, he continued. "Having said that, I'm not entirely sure if I can help you. With you being a minor, the scope of my representation is quite limited."

A-ha. It must be the money.

"It's the fee, isn't it? I have some money."

He smiled a warm smile. "No, that's not it at all. It's just that..."

Brian Thompson didn't actually stop speaking, I'd just stopped listening. I was watching the new boy. And he was looking at me. The new boy was looking at me. *Do I have something on my face? Did I spill my lunch on my T-shirt?* No, my lunch was still sitting in its tray, untouched. The new boy, Turner, arched an eyebrow, with an ever-so-slight nod to my future attorney. He was asking me a question. I gave him a shoulder shrug. The smile I got in return made me feel all warm.

Brian Thompson, Attorney-at-Law, was looking at me. He'd stopped talking and waited for me to respond. Sadly, I had no idea what he'd asked, so I just winged it. "Yeah, that will be fine," I said nodding my head.

"Great," he said as he got to his feet. "Let's go. It can't hurt to try."

I was confused as I stood up, looking down at my untouched lunch. Oh well, there's always dinner. Dumping my tray, I followed my attorney out the door. Where were we going? Taking a glance back at the new boy, he was still looking at me with those eyes of his.

Hmmm.

"Miss Hill, where are the camp offices?" Mr. Thompson asked when we get outside. I pointed to the University Center, starting to get a clue. It may take a moment sometimes, but I get up to speed pretty darn quick.

"My being here may seem unusual," Mr. Thompson began as we walked in the afternoon sunshine, "but I have a teenage daughter who hasn't talked to me since her mother and I divorced. She wanted space and I let her have it. Lots of it. I was angry and pushed her away. Every day I regret letting my daughter go the way I did. You'll find as you get older it's the regrets that haunt you." He looked straight ahead with the air of a man wishing he could go back and change things. "So when you called, I knew I had to see if I could help you. I don't know if I can, but if there's one thing I'm good at, it's creating a stink."

The coming confrontation got my heart pounding. It was going to be fun watching my vicious attorney take on the crabby camp administrator. In a cage match between the two, I'd put my money on the blood-sucking attorney every time. After all, he went to law school to study intimidation and browbeating, right?

I followed my wolf across the lobby. An administrator waited like an unsuspecting sheep behind the counter. Let the games begin.

"I'm Brian Thompson, Attorney-at-Law. I'm here to assist my client, Miss Hill." He gestures in my direction.

Filled with pride, I found myself standing a little taller as I took in a deep breath.

"Is there someplace we can talk?" Mr. Thompson asked.

The man pointed to the nearby seating area and we followed him. The man leaned back in his chair, arms folded, clearly defiant. He didn't offer a word but just continued glaring at my attorney. I glanced at Mr. Thompson, and he gave me a reassuring smile.

"Miss Hill has been registered at the wrong camp. She does not have a criminal record in the juvenile court system and has been an exemplary student at her school."

True; I do get good grades.

Leaning back, Brian Thompson, Attorney-at-Law, continued. "Her father's intent was to register her for the Agape bible camp. A camp where she could get closer to God, study the bible, and be an inspiration to her peers."

Inspiration? That might be a little farfetched, but I was okay with it.

"Miss Hill was not meant to be at this boot camp. Her father would want her to be at the right camp." That's what I told him, only not nearly as persuasively.

"Mr. Thompson," the man began, "Our bible camp ended last week, so there isn't even an option to transfer her to another of our camps. Also, I have her online registration form, completed by Miss Hill's father, signing her up for this camp, Camp ToughLove." He pushed a printout across the table. Neither of us bothered to pick it up.

"Unless you can present one of her parents, I am not authorized to release her. As an attorney, you must realize the liability we could expose ourselves to if we released Miss Hill based solely on her word alone. Despite the good we bring to our camp attendees, most do not want to be here. Camp ToughLove is not an easy summer vacation playing video games and hanging out with friends. Our campers work hard to develop their character. Miss Hill would not be the first to attempt to leave our boot camp. Though I have to say she certainly has been the most creative."

Mr. Thompson looked at me, the question implicit. I sighed. "My father is unreachable. And my mother has been missing for three years now. I have no other relatives I could call. Apparently, it's just me." Out of the corner of my eye, I spotted Turner, the new boy walking with our group, headed for the auditorium. My eyes tracked him until he was out of sight.

I stood up. "I guess I'll just have to stay here and make the best of it. I better run and catch up to my group." Turning back to Brian Thompson, Attorney-at-Law, I held out my hand. "Thanks for trying. I'm glad you were here to help me."

As I'd seen a little ray of light in the camp, I wasn't going to fight my forced stay. No doubt leaving a pair of confused and relieved adults behind me, I turned to run after my group—and the new boy.

Bow chicka wow wow.

10
It's Not Easy Being Green

Stacia and I were taking a shortcut through the long grass on the way to meet with our counselors when I felt something squishy under my bare feet. I grabbed Stacia's arm, pulling her to a stop.

"What?" she asked.

"Don't you feel it? It's sort of like mud, only slimier."

Stacia bent down and moaned. "Oh man." She is staring at something on the ground.

"What?" I asked. As I got no response, I squatted down—and was absolutely horrified.

There were dead frogs everywhere. Literally thousands of dead frogs littered the ground. I even had one sticking up between my toes. I'd swear they weren't here when we started on the shortcut.

"Ughh," I gasped, lifting my foot. When I put it back down, another frog squished. Reflexively jerking my foot back up, I lost balance and put it down harder, this time mashing a dead frog into the ground with my heel.

We looked at each other, totally grossed out beyond measure. Stacia was going green, and I knew it was only a matter of seconds before she started barfing. We had to get out of there, fast. I reached for her hand, desperate in my attempt to both comfort and be comforted.

"No, don't look," I said as Stacia made the mistake of looking down again. Horrified, she jumped back, pulling me off balance. Unbelievably things got worse—we toppled over. Stacia landed on her back while I'd landed on top of her. Stacia started to scream and thrash. "No, stop!" I yelled as we rolled over.

At a party last Halloween, I'd been blindfolded and put my hand into cold spaghetti believing with all of my being that I was touching the intestines of some dead guy. This was far worse. The cold, slimy bodies of the dead frogs pressed into my back, creating a panic I would never forget.

"Girls," a woman's calming voice called out across the field.

I stopped my scream before it left my throat. Wrapped up in each other's arms, we continued to thrash, trying desperately not to be the one on the ground. Trying not to be the one who touched the dead frog bodies.

"Girls," the voice called again.

We still hung onto each other but stopped our struggling. "Help each other. Get to your feet and move this way." I gave Stacia a push to help her get up.

"That's it, now help her up, too," the woman instructed.

Stacia slowly reached down, terror haunting her eyes. Clutching her hand, I got to my feet. The frogs were still underneath my feet, but it was light-years better than having them touching my body.

"Move this way," she commanded.

I was finally able to look in her direction. A woman with medium brown hair stood on the sidewalk. Recognizing her as Mrs. Bies, the science teacher, I took a tentative step towards her.

Stacia took a small step forward and stopped. A moan escaped her lips.

I grabbed her hand and shouted, "Run!"

Together, we sprinted the last 20 yards, crashing into Mrs. Bies when we reached safety. Still freaked out beyond measure, I ran my hands over my legs trying to get any frog remains off my body. Stacia was bent over, heaving her guts up onto the sidewalk. I was trying to catch my breath, wanting to push my panic as far away as I could. That was absolutely horrible.

"What killed all those frogs?" I asked Mrs. Bies. My voice sounded ragged, not at all like my normal voice. "I have never seen anything like that. It was so incredibly gross."

Stacia looked up. "I have to agree. Very gross." She spat out the last of her vomit as if to punctuate her point. I had to laugh, as there wasn't anything else I could do. Disgusting.

Mrs. Bies put a hand on Stacia's shoulder. "I've studied biology for years and have never come across anything like this. There have been mass wildlife deaths, but they're typically near a polluted stream or pond. However, this is a university campus, not an industrial facility. We shouldn't be near any of the sort of chemicals which could cause a mass kill like this." She looked perplexed.

I had a question. "It's not just the killing that's odd, but is it normal for this many frogs to gather in a field like this? There have to be thousands here, and the nearest pond or river is a half-mile away. What would bring them here—just to kill them off? And it had to happen relatively fast, as I haven't seen a single dead frog beyond the bordering sidewalks."

Mrs. Bies looked around, a frown on her face. "I don't get it, but I'm going to make a few calls to search for answers. We have to make sure there aren't any contaminants on campus that could potentially harm the students. This is so odd," she said, shaking her head. "I hope you two are going to be okay."

I glanced over at Stacia, who was looking better—at least she'd lost the green color. It wasn't her shade anyway. "I think the worst is over," I told her, but deep down I wondered if that was true.

"Cruel Summer" was a song by the Eighties group, Bananarama —a band name that always made me think that all the good names were gone. But, I could relate to the girl left on her own to survive, except for in the song, the girl suffered from the heat. No dead frogs anywhere.

🐾

INSIDE THE WYMAN CENTER, Stacia and I separated to meet with our counselors. Apparently, as a troubled teen, I needed to meet regularly with a counselor to keep me on the right path. The right path? If they only knew. Not only did I stay on the right path, I owned the path.

Ms. Neuman, the well-dressed counselor who spoke at our gathering on the subject of personal responsibility, turned out to be my counselor. Maybe I could learn some things about fashion from her, but if she was going to talk to me about personal responsibility, I'd heard it. New subject, please.

I was beckoned into an office and waved over to a chair across from Ms. Neuman. She sat back, crossed her legs and jotted a note on a pad. I studied her fashionable heels while she kept me waiting. Finally, she looked up. "What would you like to talk about today, Abbey?"

Really, it was up to me? Okay, then. Dead frogs it was. "What's up with the dead frogs? Aren't frogs like a canary in a coal mine? You know, a low-tech early warning system that shouts, 'danger, danger.' Is this camp unsafe? Should I be worried? Do I need to call my lawyer?"

Based on the blank look Ms. Neuman displayed, I guessed this wasn't the direction she'd been expecting. Could I help it if my mind wasn't wired like everyone else's? She rolled with it though and asked a follow-up question without hesitation. "If you could clarify, that would be most helpful. Is dead frogs a ghetto expression or are you referring to actual dead frogs?"

Ghetto expression? I lived in Woodbury for heaven's sake. Our cheerleaders were named Buffy and Madison. We had a Trader Joe's and a Pier One. A soccer mom drove the only Escalade in the entire suburb. We were the polar opposite of ghetto.

"Um, no. I'm talking real dead frogs, with real dead frog guts squishing between your toes. Stacia and I cut through the field outside and there were thousands of frogs lying there just dead. And they weren't no drive-by shooting victims, either." I used my best MTV gangster-sounding voice for the last line. Her look of irritation led me to believe I may have crossed the line a wee bit. Oh well.

"I'll have maintenance look into it."

I was hoping for more of a rise out of her. "Is this place haunted?" I continued. "I've heard a few construction workers discussing some strange happenings here. It's more than dead frogs, isn't it? Are there ghosts in your camp?" That should do it.

Ms. Neuman lowered her notepad. She fixed me with a look of exasperation—a look I feel I'd seen before. "I realize you're seeking attention here, Miss Hill. Many of the inner city kids are missing a parent, which would certainly justify your search for attention and validation."

Huh? Inner city?

"However, I have a professional responsibility to clear up your apparent misunderstanding. There are no such things as ghosts. The people who see ghosts are uneducated, delusional and weak minded. These are the same people who visit a psychic asking their dead Aunt Martha what numbers to play in the lottery. Abbey, just because the uneducated and street people surround you, doesn't mean you need to buy into their delusions. If you're ever going to rise above your current situation, you will need to have a sharp mind. If something doesn't make sense to you, reject it."

I already had. Standing up, I asked, "Where are you from, Ms. Neuman?"

Confusion written on her face, it took a moment for her to answer. "I live in Stillwater. It's a charming little town located near —" I held up a hand, stopping her in mid-sentence.

"I know where Stillwater is. I live in Woodbury, just two towns over from Stillwater. Woodbury is not the inner city and it's not the ghetto. The only white trash we have is the newspapers on recycling day. I suggest you prepare a tad bit more before our next meeting."

Maybe this counseling stuff worked. I walked out feeling much better than when I arrived.

11

GHOSTS OF GRANDMOTHERS PAST

"She doesn't believe in Santa Claus or the Easter Bunny. And I'm pretty sure she doesn't believe in the Pilgrims either." I told Stacia about Ms. Neuman's refusal to believe in something she couldn't see. "People see ghosts all the time."

"All the time?"

"At least I see them all the time."

Stacia looked at me warily. "You do?"

"Well, maybe not *all* the time," I backpedaled. "But Ms. Neuman was way off base on a lot of things. She kept assuming I was from the ghetto. Stacia, are all you troubled teens from the inner city?"

Stacia laughed. "Hardly. But, us suburban kids have our issues too."

"Not me. I don't have any issues."

"Uh-huh," she said, a grin on her face. "What color is the sky in your world?"

"Blue," I replied smugly. "Except it's a brighter blue than you're used to seeing. You should visit sometime."

Stacia shook her head. "And people say I'm the strange one in my family," she muttered.

As we walked through the first floor of Grimm Hall, Stacia said, "Brr, it feels cold right here." She had her arms wrapped around herself. "Don't you feel that?" she asked.

"Yeah, it's a cold spot." I shrugged. "But what's the big deal? I notice them all the time. Don't you?"

She stopped and stared at me. "Abbey, that's not normal."

LOCATED in one of the oldest buildings on campus, our science classroom had creaking wooden floors, and a certain mustiness you'll never find in buildings built within the last 100 years. Sitting in the back, I listened as Charlotte Bies introduced the class.

"Edwin Hubble said that, equipped with his five senses, man explores the universe around him and calls the adventure science. One of the most critical skills in science is that of observation. Most of the time we think of observation as something we do with our eyes; when we see something, we observe it."

Mrs. Bies walked down the center aisle, making eye contact with many of the students. "In fact, Yogi Berra famously said you could observe a lot just by watching. However, all five of our senses can be used to make observations: sight, hearing, taste, touch, and smell. And with those, we can make two kinds of observation: those that are facts, and those that are opinions. Facts are those things that are true for everybody. Opinions are beliefs based on personal preference. But that's just my opinion."

At last, a teacher with a sense of humor. It's so much better than Mr. Johnson and his rope climbing marathon in the gym.

Mrs. Bies had us close our eyes and handed each of us an object. After a moment, she took back the object while we jotted down our observations of the object based solely on our sense of touch. Then with our eyes closed again, she handed back the object to use our sense of hearing as we unwrapped the object. Next, with our eyes opened we used our sense of sight to observe the object. After making our notes we were told, "Now use your sense of smell to observe the object." Finally, Mrs. Bies asked us to place the object in our mouth and use our sense of taste to observe it. And just to be sure, I tasted two more. So far, the thing I liked most about science is the chocolate truffles.

After class, I waited for everyone to leave and then made my way up front to talk to Mrs. Bies. "Excuse me, Mrs. Bies," I tentatively began.

"After what we've been through, call me Charlotte. How are you, Abbey?" She had a concerned look as she held my gaze. "Have you recovered from the trauma of the frog kill? That was horrible."

"Tell me about it. You didn't have frog guts between your toes. It was gross."

"I can only imagine. The Department of Natural Resources said they were sending someone out to investigate. I'll let you know what they discover. Though I can't see how there would be any contaminates on campus which could be so deadly."

"Maybe it wasn't a contaminant." I just put it out there.

Charlotte paused, one hand still in her briefcase. "Go on."

"There could have been another cause—a cause science doesn't recognize." I paused, taking a deep breath. "This camp is certainly an unusual place. Let me ask you this: have you encountered anything out of the ordinary during your time here?"

Pulling her hand back out of the briefcase, Charlotte leaned against the desk. She folded her arms, looking at me. "Besides 10,000 dead frogs?"

I nodded. "Besides 10,000 dead frogs."

A sigh. Charlotte looked to be having an internal struggle. "I was working late two nights ago, logging some research time on a pet project. I live in an older house here on campus. I was alone upstairs with the door closed, no one else in the house. Unbelievably, at 12:15 a.m., I heard footsteps coming up the stairs to the landing just outside my door. The doors were locked, so no one should have been inside. Yet, I heard someone making their way upstairs."

Charlotte brushed back her hair and continued. "The footsteps stopped right outside my door. There was no place for the person to go, other than back down to the main floor. I called out, asking who was there. No answer was given, so I pulled open the door. Of course, no one was waiting there. I had clearly heard footsteps coming up the wooden stairs, so why hadn't I heard them retreat down the steps? I was determined to get to the bottom of things, and I searched the entire house. The doors were still locked—including the door chain— and no one was hiding inside the house. Believe me, I was quite thorough." She shook her head. "I have no explanation for what happened—I just hope it doesn't happen again."

I held Charlotte's gaze as I asked the hard question. "Do you believe in ghosts?"

"Science doesn't believe in ghosts."

"Nice try, but it doesn't answer the question. Do *you* believe in ghosts?"

"I am all about the science, so I can't separate my feelings and beliefs from what science offers: cold, reasoning facts. Ghosts are anecdotal. They are stories getting repeated over campfires, stories not amounting to anything more than what someone thought they saw."

As I knew a few things about ghosts, I felt the need to set Charlotte straight. "But what about the sheer number of people who have seen something? Ghosts, spirits, poltergeists, call them what you will, people are seeing these things. I've seen them."

There, I've said it—no going back now. I've learned the hard way not to be so open when it came to my ghostly experiences. Being ridiculed publicly as the ghost girl had taught me to keep my mouth shut.

Charlotte nodded. "The thing is, almost everyone knows someone who has seen a ghost. The stories are everywhere, yet science doesn't believe. Science says there is no proof. Science looks for reproducible results that will either prove or disprove a hypothesis. And the trouble is, it's all random sightings, just anecdotal evidence. No one can prove there are ghosts."

I shook my head. "I can."

Charlotte looked surprised. "You can?" Clearly not believing.

I nodded and moved toward the stairs. Looking up the darkened staircase, I called, "Edith." I said nothing further and continued watching the staircase. Waiting.

It began with a creak—as if weight was being placed on the old wooden steps. Charlotte watched the stairs, her sense of expectation palpable. It happened again, closer this time. Charlotte strained to see into the shadows. I heard it again, the creak louder still. Charlotte's hand touched my arm. The sound was now right there. If I'd closed my eyes, I would have sworn on a very tall stack of bibles someone had made their way down the staircase and was in the room with us.

Charlotte looked around nervously as the wooden floorboards creaked under the weight of something neither of us could see. But, there was a presence in the room.

It was difficult to explain what I was feeling. It was a tingling, an energy that reminded me of the static electricity buildup I got when shuffled my feet on the carpet in the dry winter months. This ghostly presence didn't scare me, however. The feeling was warm, a gentle stirring in my soul, that brought back the lush feeling of climbing into my grandma's lap when I was a little girl. It was funny, but briefly— two breathes at most—I smelled grandma's perfume and recognized it right away. You know how old ladies have their favorite perfume? Grandma's was White Shoulders. It was a smell I would always remember.

Charlotte had to be feeling the presence as well—the hairs on her arm were standing up. "Who is Edith?" she asked with a deer-in-the-headlights look. "You called out her name, and then..." Charlotte shivered.

"Edith was my grandmother. She used to hold me in her lap and read me stories when I was a lot younger. I loved her more than anything." The thing was, I knew she was nearby. Call it intuition or some paranormal sense, but I could feel her. There are some things you just know, right?

"Are you telling me your dead grandmother was in the room, here with us?"

"Well, maybe. I can't explain it, but the feeling reminded me of her. So I used her name and someone nice joined us. She had a familiar feeling, a comforting one. Just like being with my grandma."

Charlotte held up her hand. "I didn't see anyone."

"Neither did I." I held her gaze.

"But someone came down the stairs. I heard it. Someone was here with us, I could feel her." Charlotte paused. She had tears rolling down her cheeks. "And it was a *her*. I distinctly felt something feminine in the room with us. I wasn't scared. Okay, maybe a little at first, but once I sensed her, it felt oddly comforting. Was that a ghost, Abbey?"

I nodded. "I've grown up with experiences like this all of my life. Over the years, I've learned I could make contact with these spirits. You were talking about reproducible results. So what does this do for science?"

"I, for one, have become a believer. However, I'm concerned about you. Are you safe from the effects of this activity?" Charlotte frowned and worry flashed across her face. "Wait, suppose it's you? What if you are the catalyst for this type of activity? Did the frog kill happen because of you?"

I shook my head vigorously. "I'm normal. Or about as normal as a 14-year-old teenager can be. Things just happen around me, that's all. You can't really believe I caused those frogs to die," I pleaded with Charlotte. I could feel my eyes threatening to tear up. I didn't want to cry.

She shook her head. "No, Abbey, I don't. You are a sweet girl. Not at all the sort of child to summon up an evil, frog-killing demon." She gave me a warm smile, making me feel better—at least until her smile was replaced by a frown.

I followed her stare. A blood-red symbol had appeared on the wall behind me. This symbol was not there earlier. It looked like a fancy lowercase letter F, except the top part was reversed.

While we stared at the symbol, a dot appeared in the lower right, like this:

"What does it mean?" I asked.

Charlotte shook her head. "I'm not the one to ask. Maybe you should be asking Edith."

"I can't say it was my grandmother with 100 percent certainty. There aren't a lot of certainties where I'm concerned."

"That's for certain," Charlotte said with a smile. "I can't believe we are talking ghosts and facts within the same sentence."

I shrugged. "Our world is a much bigger place than science believes. Did you know when Shakespeare wrote, 'There are more things in heaven and earth, Horatio, than are dreamt of in your philosophy,' he was referring to a ghost?"

Charlotte didn't answer as we watched the symbol fade into the wall. The dot was the last part to disappear.

12

AIN'T NO MOUNTAIN
HIGH ENOUGH

I t felt like a Monday, but since it was summer, I had no idea what day it really was.

I stared at the ceiling, not wanting to face the day. This place had taken a decidedly weird turn. And that was saying a lot coming from Abnormally Abbey, the princess of weird. Things happen to me that don't happen to ordinary people.

For example, just a week or so before my mother disappeared, something happened. We had recently moved into an older farmhouse on the outer edge of Woodbury. After everyone had gone to bed, I was lying in mine, having trouble sleeping. I heard footsteps moving down the hall. As they got to my wide open door, my cat—who had been staring at the open door—got rigid and tense all of a sudden. Lulu made a deep throaty hissing noise I had never heard her make before, as her hair stood straight up and her cat nails dug into my sheets. I reached to comfort her and she bolted from the room at my touch. After Lulu was gone, I had more time to process what had come in.

It looked like a dark shade of fog in human shape. It was hardly noticeable in the air except for the outlines of movement as it walked. I could see most clearly near its hips, distinctly making out legs as it walked across my room. It moved parallel to the end of my bed, to the corner near my closet. I only saw the outline for probably ten seconds —though it felt much longer—but it was long enough to feel the full weight of what was in the room with me. But all I could do was clench my teeth and sit anxiously while I continued to hear small noises coming from that part of the room. I had the feeling he didn't want to be seen or acknowledged; he was simply trying to get out of his room after my parents had occupied it. I pulled the covers up, trying to hide. Eventually, I fell asleep.

The following night, I'd just gone to bed when I saw the tall, black transparent figure again walk through my door from the hallway. That's when I heard strange scratching noises on my wall from the corner. I had no doubt there was something there, but I didn't want to deal with it, possibly waking up my parents. Instead, I quietly crept out, went downstairs and curled up on the couch in front of the fireplace. In the morning, I went back to my room and looked at the wall. There were faint marks etched on my wall where I heard the scratching. Like most things I saw, I kept it to myself. I didn't want to be "that crazy girl." I wanted to be normal like everyone else.

Except I'm *not* normal, and it was getting more and more difficult to hide that fact.

"Hey, Mom," I said hoping somehow to connect with her. "Hope you're not having a Manic Monday. It sure feels like one. I'm worried about not being normal. Will they think I'm out of this world when they learn what I can do? Remember the Eighties song 'The Safety Dance' by Men Without Hats? I loved the spirit behind it. We can go where we want and act like we want, because it's safe to dance. Maybe I shouldn't worry about what others think. Because if they can't dance, then they're no friends of mine."

I was almost embarrassed talking to my mother this way, but it still helped.

I JOINED our physical training group on the obstacle course. Mr. Johnson gave me a look that said 'I'm watching your every step' as I got in the back of the line. All I could do was shrug. The group was ready to start the course, but Mr. Johnson held up his hand stopping the first girl from starting.

"Miss Hill, why don't you go first today?"

Several responses came to mind, but I wisely kept them to myself.

"Let me give you a warning: if you are too slow, the group will have to run the course a second time," he threatened.

Groans erupted from the group. My reputation for speed preceded me.

Making my slow journey to the front of the line, I got several elbows along the way. I was clearly destined not to be popular. At the head of the line, Carrie gave me a look. "You better move your butt," she snarled. "I was supposed to lead the group today."

"There's always tomorrow," I told her, trying to sound more flippant than I felt.

"Could you move any slower?" Carrie taunted.

"Whatever." Why is it I always met up with a mean girl no matter where I went? Life was never fair.

"Go," Mr. Johnson commanded. I went.

I felt Carrie's hand on my back giving me a shove. Rather than propelling me, it caused me to stumble. I was able to get my hands down, saving me from the embarrassment of a very public face plant. Getting to my feet, I pushed off as we raced for the tires, the first obstacle. The tires were laid out in a grid pattern and I figured out the secret was to take exaggerated steps, lifting my knees high like a country music dancer. It looked silly, but it worked. I was through just as Carrie got to the tires behind me. She was gaining on me rapidly, though.

Tunnels were the next obstacle I had to endure. It looked as if they brought in sewer pipes for us to crawl through. The concrete was murder on my knees, so I crab walked my way down the tunnel. Carrie was right behind now. "Move," she shouted at me, the sound echoing down the tunnel. Daylight was ahead and I was out.

A steep climbing wall was up next. Wide enough for several of us to climb at the same time, multiple ropes were hanging down. I cut off Carrie to grab the closest one. Just like gym class, I gripped and pulled, gripped and pulled. Glancing to my right, I discover I was actually moving up the rope faster than Carrie. This spiked my adrenaline and I became a machine, never tiring as I made my way up the wall.

At the top, I looked over the side at the steep slide and I was paralyzed. I hate heights. Carrie caught up and with little regard for her safety, threw herself over the edge. My hands shaking, I just couldn't do it.

"Take my hand," a boy's voice offered. I glanced up to find Turner holding out his hand. "We'll go down together."

Numbly, I grabbed his hand and off we went. I shrieked as we rocketed down the brushed metal surface, with nothing to slow us down. A pile of sand broke our fall at the bottom. Not exactly a graceful landing, I landing hard and pitched forward onto my belly.

Right by my outstretched hand, I spotted Carrie's glasses. She also had a hard landing and was on her hands and knees searching for her glasses—the ones that were in my hand. Turner tugged me up by my other hand, encouraging me to continue.

"Hang on," I told him and held out Carrie's glasses for her. "Here they are," I said. She looked at me for the briefest of moments, not saying a word and took them from me. Clearly not overly sentimental, she was up and moving for the next obstacle without saying a word of thanks.

Whatever.

Still holding Turner's hand, we raced for the pylon obstacle. Imagine some very short telephone poles driven into the ground. At the obstacle's start, the pylons were placed low and close together. Once they were surrounded by a muddy bog, the pylons got higher and spread out—far enough that you could no longer step across, you had to jump from one to the other. To make things more difficult, the pylons weren't in a straight line. They were arranged so you had to jump to your left, then to your right and then back to the left. The zigzag pattern continued until the end. If you slipped or missed your jump, a mud bath was your reward. Way too much fun to have before breakfast.

Turner gestured for me to step up on the first pylon. A glance to my right showed me Carrie was already onto her third pylon on the other set. I stepped up and moved across the short distance to the next pylon. A bit more of a stretch to reach up to the third one, and not being the tallest girl, getting to the third pylon meant a small jump up. Arms outstretched for balance, I hopped up to the top of the pylon, which was just large enough for both my feet.

Wobbly and fighting for balance, I sized up my next leap.

This one was to my left, and a good foot higher and six inches further than the last. Feet together, I crouched and jumped. My forward momentum almost took me headfirst off the pylon. This near plunge taught me I should jump with one foot at a time—sort of like crossing a creek by leaping from stone to stone.

The fifth pylon was to my right. I turned, orienting my body for the jump. This pylon followed the same pattern: a little higher and a little farther.

Carrie was still several ahead of me. Making her leap, Carrie's technique was to reach her foot toward her target and then push off with her back leg. Built like a soccer player, her legs looked strong and her leaps required little of the effort that mine did. Though she didn't exactly stick her landing, Carrie's balance was better than mine.

A question popped into my head. What would happen if I were to actually jump from post to post just like crossing a creek? Go big or not at all, right? I took a moment to size it up. Deep breath. Go! I jumped to my right, landing on my right foot and then immediately jumped to my left, landing on my left foot. So far so good. I pushed off, repeating the process, again and again. It worked; I was now even with Carrie.

Glancing over at me, Carrie's look of determination—she clearly didn't want to lose—was totally evident on her face. Tough bananas. I jumped off, finding my rhythm easily and started to pull ahead of her. I heard a four-letter word from Carrie, who was now in second place.

Ah, satisfaction.

My legs were beginning to feel like rubber as I saw the end approach. Just two more pylons to go, then a longer jump off the last one to take me past the mud bog and a 20-yard sprint to the finish. I was definitely going to beat her.

Several things happen as we grow up. Our body begins to mature and we get a little faster and a little stronger. Mentally, we are also maturing. We learn lessons from what life throws at us. In step with losing some of our childlike innocence, was the realization not all of life will go as we have planned. I did not beat Carrie.

Pausing on the final pylon, I sized up my last—and longest—leap. *I can do this.* Deep breath in, I grunted loudly with the effort of my jump. My legs strode in mid-air as I flew. Landing awkwardly, I pitched to the side. I had a mouthful of sand, as I seemed to have landed face first. Carrie jumped right after me, sticking her landing and raced off for the finish line.

Determination lit my inner fire and I was on my feet, spitting out sand, as I pumped my arms attempting to catch up to her. I was able to get close and made a last second dive as we got to the finish line. It wasn't enough though, as she beat me. However—and this was the important part—I was close. When I first got to camp, I never would have guessed I'd be able to keep up with someone like Carrie. I almost beat her. Even though my self-confidence soared, I still wasn't ready to admit this camp might be a good thing. That was, until...

"That was impressive," Turner said, holding out a strong hand as he brought me to my feet effortlessly. My hand lingered in his, my eyes holding his. His smile was enough to bring my heart rate racing like I was right back on the obstacle course. Only this time, I was right where I wanted to be.

13

BAD GIRLS

"I'm from deep in the South where sushi is still called bait," Truly said on our way back from breakfast. She wore the same blue sweater I first saw her in.

"I don't see much of you around camp. Where do you hang out?"

"Been busier than a one eyed cat watching three mouse holes." And then shrugging, Truly said with a vague smile, "I've been around."

Having read of the Cheshire cat's smile in Alice in Wonderland, I suspected I wasn't getting the whole story when I saw Truly's smile. I was going to have to keep my eye on her. Never trust the south, I always say.

WE WENT our separate ways as we entered Grimm Hall. I decided showering would be a good thing before lunch. The combination of sweat, dirt and sand would take away even the strongest of appetites. Besides, Turner should be there at lunch, too.

I headed for the shower wanting to be done before Stacia came back. As I stood under the hot stream of water, I was stretching my sore arms when it occurred to me I could actually see some muscle. I straightened my arm and noticed the back of my arm tighten up. I didn't think that muscle was there before. Nice. I held up my arms flexing my biceps. *I may not be a plumber, but I sure got pipes.* I tried a different pose. *With these sick puppies, I should go see the vet.*

A nearby giggle pulled me from my fantasy world. Maybe in the land of community showers, it may be best if I held off on trying out my bodybuilder poses. It was just such a unique experience to finally have some muscles as I hadn't always been the most active girl in the world. I grabbed my towel and looked around to find the source of the giggle. Of course, it had to be Carrie. I hightailed it out of there.

I FELT a hand on my shoulder as I opened the door to my room. It was Stacia. "Where have you been?" I asked her.

"I ran into Truly and we got to talking," Stacia said, her eyes sliding down. "Nice towel, by the way." I was wrapped in the tropical bird towel my mom had brought me from one of her South America trips.

"Yeah, thanks. I saw Truly as well. I always get the feeling that she's up to something."

"You never can tell with her," Stacia said. "She is a smart one. And you know how dangerous that can be." Laughing, she plopped down on her bed.

I was just about ready to make my bed, when I saw it. The same symbol Charlotte and I saw last night was on my sheet. It was as if someone had used a finger to draw the symbol right there on my sheet. It was a delicate impression, but the morning light hit it just right so I could see it.

But I was stunned. What did it mean?

"Stacia, come have a look at this."

She leaned over my shoulder. "Look at what? Did you wet the bed?"

I gave Stacia an elbow. "What do you make of this?" I asked tracing my finger over the symbol on my bed sheet.

"I don't know what it is," she said. "Did you draw it?"

I shook my head. "I found it this way. It's like someone drew it on my sheet. Even odder, it's the same symbol Charlotte and I saw on the wall of her office last night. It was so strange, the mark faded away while we were looking at it. And then it was gone altogether."

"It's fading away here too." The line traced onto my sheet was disappearing as we watched. "Our door was locked, wasn't it?" Stacia asked with a shudder.

I nodded. "But, what could it mean? I have zero idea."

"Me neither," Stacia said. "I wish you could call and ask whoever drew this."

"I have a feeling the person responsible for the message is not in a place to receive my call." I gave a dramatic pause. "If you know what I mean."

Stacia's arms were wrapped around herself, as she shuddered again. "Yeah, I think I know what you mean."

LUNCH. The downside of my existence at camp. The food was worse than any greasy spoon truck stop I'd ever had the dubious pleasure of visiting. The atmosphere was decidedly unfriendly, and the hostile looks I got reminded me of a Survivor tribe sizing up their opponent right before they slam them to the ground and trample them in the latest reward challenge. I needed to make some alliances here if I was going to survive.

To make matters worse, getting to the cafeteria late meant not having much of a choice where to sit. With all of the cliques, choosing the wrong table could be dangerous. I didn't see either Stacia or Truly and I didn't feel confident enough to approach Turner. So I stood in place with my tray, paralyzed with indecision. The pressure was far worse than I would have guessed.

"Excuse me," a voice said. My trance was broken by the boy appearing at my side. A tall boy with reddish blonde hair, he wore a red shirt with Gunners written across his broad chest. He was dressed in athletic shorts and soccer cleats.

I smiled and excused myself.

The smile I got in return took my breath away. "Let me ask you a quick question. How much does a polar bear weigh?" He didn't wait for my answer. "Just enough to break the ice." He flashed a big grin and gave me an appraising look. "I like you, come join us for lunch."

Nodding at the amazingly large pile of food on his tray, I say, "Clearly, you've never tried the food here. It's really quite awful."

"When you're as hungry as I am, it's all good." Gently placing a hand on the small of my back, he guided me toward an empty table away from the rest of our camp. This was one smooth operator. I liked him, even if he was a little cheesy.

I took the offered seat and he sat across from me. The rest of the table was almost immediately filled with his friends.

"I'm Tommy," he offered. He held my eye, a confident grin on his face. Most boys would be asking my name, or at the least, trying to fill the silence. Not this one.

I was the first to give in. "My name is Abbey."

"A beautiful name." Without breaking eye contact, he grabbed a carrot stick and took a noisy bite.

"You're new here, aren't you?" I asked. "I haven't seen you before." Tommy and I were the only ones talking. The boys at the table took in our exchange, watching us while they ate. It was like being under a spotlight.

A nod. "Our soccer camp started today. It runs through Saturday. Three glorious days of fun in the sun. We're all staying at McMillan Hall and sharing this five-star dining experience with your camp." This got a laugh from the other boys. "What about you, Abbey? What are you here for?"

He really should be asking what I was *in* for. Honesty is best, right? "I'm here at Camp ToughLove."

Some of the other boys choked on their food. I got a raised eyebrow from Tommy. "Are you a *bad* girl, Abbey?" I didn't appreciate the emphasis he gave to the word bad.

"Look, I was sent to the wrong camp. My father thought he was dropping me off at a church camp, and he's out on assignment and totally unreachable. So now I'm stuck here with the troubled teens in this haunted place." I may have said too much, judging by the looks I received.

"Haunted?" Tommy asked.

Biting my bottom lip, I nodded.

"Really?" Tommy looked at me like I just reached over and helped myself to a handful of his mashed potatoes.

"It's okay if you don't believe me," I said as I stood. "I should be going."

Tommy was out of his chair in a heartbeat. "Abbey, please stay. Don't leave me here alone with this lot," gesturing to the other boys at the table. "For what it's worth, I believe you." I looked into his eyes and seeing only sincerity, I sat.

"Can I see your cell phone?" he asked.

I slid it over, unsure of what he was up to. What I was enjoying was the fact that he was up to something and I was the center of his attention. It reminded me of what I'd been missing since my father left. What a girl finds so special about her father is she's the focus of his loving attention. A girl knows her father is interested in everything about her and most importantly, he isn't judging. My father loves me for all my quirks, all my faults and even all my bad fashion choices. I missed him.

Why am I sitting in front of this über-confident boy, fighting back tears as I thought of my father?

Tommy held up my phone, smiling broadly and took a picture of himself. He slid it back. "I added my number, so call anytime. If you need anything, call me. Be it hauntings or ghosts, I might be able to help." He leaned back, with a smile so supremely confident, I just had to laugh.

"Girl, you know it's true," he added.

Wait, what? Did he just quote the most infamous of songs from the Eighties? "Girl You Know It's True" by Milli Vanilli was a fraud cooked up by a record producer. The artists who were on stage lip-syncing were not actually the artists who recorded the popular song. Now I wondered how genuine Tommy really was.

"All right. I'll call—if I need your help. But I should be running." I stood and took the long walk across the room, knowing his eyes were following me.

14

Don't Make Me Release the Flying Monkeys

Sitting in my bible study class, listening as the teacher spoke about the Holy Spirit got me thinking. What would he say about the spirits I see? Would he have some special insight as to why they reach out to me? After class, I decided to test the spiritual waters.

"Excuse me, Mr. Kindle. I was wondering about ghosts. Where do they fit in with theology?"

Mr. Kindle was a short man stuffed into a too small tweed sports coat with sleeves meant for someone with longer arms. He appeared to be going for the academic look with his cool guy glasses and his hair worn stylishly long. His loafers even had the prerequisite tassels.

Mr. Kindle gave me a thoughtful look as he processed my question. "Well, they do not teach you about these sorts of things in theological college. In fact, Christian theology is embarrassingly silent on the matter of ghosts. There are reasons for this. Contemporary Christian theology eschews dualisms of the soul and body. Christ, as represented in his resurrection appearances, remains embodied, not free-floating ectoplasm. The perceived wisdom about ghosts is they are eternal souls wandering on the other side of death, free from their bodies."

Mr. Kindle scratched his head. "So the theological difficulties with ghosts become evident. It's not that theologians dismiss the mysterious and inexplicable; take angels and the miracle of the virgin birth or the raising of Lazarus as examples. But ghosts—detached, ethereal, grief-stricken souls—do not find an easy place in this Christian theological account of the creation."

Mr. Kindle looked at me as if he was seeing me for the first time. "Why are you asking about ghosts?"

I wasn't entirely confident I should be sharing this, but I worried there'd be a special place in hell for those who lie to their bible study teachers.

"Ghosts have been reaching out to me. But I'm not quite sure what they want. I believe they are trying to tell me something. Have you come across this before?"

Mr. Kindle shook his head, weariness evident in his manner. He leaned on the corner of his desk. "This is not uncommon, you know. Children are seen and heard, some are even singing. Favorite aunts, uncles or even parents, are seen—usually coming to comfort those they leave behind. It is assumed, even by believers, this is proof ghosts are spirits of dead people and most mean us no harm." Arms folded across his chest, his voice crept up in volume as his passion grew.

"This is a great error," he continued, "for all ghosts, without exception, are demons. They are wicked angels, followers of Satan whose only task on this earth is to deceive and to harm. Demons are like stalking lions, watching for easy prey. And when they find someone, they pounce with a boundless and utterly vicious ferocity. Demons are not just forces—they are real creatures. Under normal circumstances, they can't be seen, but they can assume human likeness whenever they wish. This is how a friend or a favorite aunt can suddenly appear to you. Demons know what they look like, what they sound like and everything about their histories, right down to their pet names for you. So, they mimic them."

Mr. Kindle was getting louder, a notch or so away from yelling at me. He gestured emphatically with his index finger. "There is evil in our world. The Bible said Satan was banished by God to just one place. You know where that place was? Earth. If you don't believe me, just watch CNN for 20 minutes. Ghosts are never friendly, Miss Hill. They are always wicked, even if they appear to be kind. Their purpose is to make us believe they are spirits of the dead. Once they manage to delude us, they continue to hold our attention, so any belief we may have in God as presented in scripture is eroded to nothing. We are warned of this in scripture. We are told no man has ever returned from the dead, except for Jesus Christ and those he raised from the dead as special miracles."

On his feet now, Mr. Kindle moved into my space. There was definite menace in his voice. "This is not a path you should be on, Miss Hill. There is no place for these spirits in Christianity. And truth be told, I'm not entirely sure there is a place for you in my class."

Clearly dismissed, he turned his back on me. With tears running down my cheeks, I ran from the room.

Turner was the one who found me sitting on the front steps of the Wyman building. Seriously late for my counseling appointment, I couldn't face Ms. Neuman. He came ambling up with such a goofy smile that I was reminded of "Let's Hear it for the Boy" from Footloose. Turner had a definite Willard vibe going.

"You look as if someone just took your last cookie," Turner said as he sat next to me, leaning back and looking into the distance, the epitome of cool. "My father used to say if life hands you a lemon, make lemonade. But if it hands you a pickle, you should just give up —because pickle-ade is disgusting."

Okay, not the cliché I was expecting. I had to fight back a smile. I did not want to smile.

Turner wasn't one to give up, though. "Hey, sometimes my life sucks, too. So much so that my ears pop just thinking about it."

I tried not to smile, as I wallowed in self-pity, feeling sorry for myself. Didn't he get that? Instead, he got my elbow.

Laughing, Turner said, "I'm happy I can help. You looked like you needed something."

Looking at Turner, his eyes were a place where I could get seriously lost. "Thank you."

I got to my feet, a sigh escaping. "I better go see my counselor. She's probably thinking I'm out stealing the wheels off abandoned ghetto cruisers in my hood."

"You are one strange girl," he said with a grin.

I couldn't help but smile right back. Let's hear it for the boy.

"TELL ME ABOUT YOUR MOTHER, ABBEY."

Again, not what I was expecting today. Ms. Neuman had been waiting for me outside of her office. Always the vogue dresser, she wore high heel boots, jeans, a black shirt and baseball cap. I'm waved into her office, where I curled my legs underneath as I sat across from Ms. Neuman. I didn't say anything as I watched her watching me. Let the derogatory comments begin.

"Tell me about your mother, Abbey," she said again.

"My mother?" I asked, stalling for time. Ms. Neuman's face didn't give away anything.

She nodded, holding up a file folder. "I took your advice from our last meeting. My experience has been that with inner...uhh... disadvantaged youth, typically the issues stem from an absent parent. As I said, I did prepare for this meeting. And I found that you have an absent parent."

"I wouldn't say she was absent." I didn't want to have this conversation—and especially not with the insensitive Ms. Neuman. "You make it sound like she's been missing school."

She shook her head. "I'm not implying anything, Miss Hill. I'm just asking. Please tell me about your mother." Her earnest gaze made my decision for me.

"She was a beautiful lady, full of life. I miss her every day. She was a doctor and traveled with the Doctors Without Borders organization. I think our time together was so precious for each of us because she was gone for weeks or months at a time."

I glanced up at my counselor who nodded for me to continue.

"We would sit on the couch, my feet draped over her lap, and talk about nearly everything. She had such a unique way of looking at things. Mom had an energy that burned so bright, people were drawn to her. I learned so much from the stories she told when she came home from each new, exotic place. Every trip would mean a souvenir —not touristy stuff, but something handmade given to her by a patient's family. I have a wall filled with things from places like Haiti, Peru, Rwanda, Colombia, Afghanistan, the Ivory Coast and Venezuela."

Ms. Neuman held my gaze. "What happened to your mother, Abbey?"

"Her name was Katherine," I began. I hated this part. You see, I didn't know if I should say *was* or *is*. I didn't know if she was alive or...

"All I know is she went to Venezuela and never came back. She'd been down there for a little over a week of her three-week stay and was traveling through a remote area, but never made it to her destination. The State Department conducted a search but came up completely empty. She was just *gone*. We couldn't accept that she wasn't coming back home. My father went down to South America with a friend and I guess they were quite thorough, even paying off local officials. Yet the result was the same."

My tears were warm on my cheek. I didn't care if I was crying in front of this woman. I missed my mom.

I'm not sure how it happened, but I felt her arms around me. It may have been the briefest of moments, it may have been several minutes, but the comfort was nice. Don't get me wrong, though; I still didn't like this cold-hearted witch.

Awkwardly disengaging, I couldn't help but think how much I wanted this camp to be over. I really needed to go home. I don't believe it was asking too much to have a kindly man step out from behind the curtain and say to me, "Close your eyes and tap your heels together three times. And think to yourself, there's no place like home."

15

SIGN, SIGN, EVERYWHERE A SIGN

Peas are gross.

I was in the cafeteria, generally ignoring the vegetables on my plate. The meatloaf and mashed potatoes were okay, but I didn't want to eat the peas. I mean, who really likes peas? I don't know of anyone who actually enjoys the pasty feeling of peas when they squish in your mouth.

I was sitting with Truly and Renata at dinner, all the while keeping an eye on Turner, who was two tables over, and Tommy, who was across the room with his loud soccer buddies. I caught both of them looking at me.

Interesting.

Some people believe the essence of happiness is having choices available to you. Others see choices as a series of paths, living with the fear of taking the wrong path, leading to heartache and catastrophe. I'd imagine these people often become quite indecisive. Me, I look at choice as an opportunity to test the waters, discover which flavor I prefer. My favorite ice cream shop lets me try spoonful after spoonful before I decide. And that's how life should be.

"Abbey, are you even listening to us?" I glanced over to Renata. No, I hadn't been listening at all.

"Sorry, I was a bit distracted." I simply gave a nod toward Tommy.

"I can see why," Truly said, giving Tommy a look over. He smiled and stood up. He obviously saw her attention as an invitation to visit our table. "Oh, he's coming over. What a charming gentleman he is."

"Hi, Abbey," a voice said to my side. It was Turner.

The only problem with trying several flavors at the ice cream shop is you don't want to intermingle more than one. Not all flavors go well together. In fact, mixing flavors can be a very bad thing.

Tommy confidently made his way across the cafeteria. This could get ugly. Turner leaned on the table waiting for my undivided attention. I gave it to him.

"Turner. What are you doing? Don't you hate these peas? I know I do." Good God, I was babbling like a complete idiot.

"Hi, Abbey. Hi, girls," Tommy said when he got to our table. He held each of our gazes for a long moment, but paused when he got to Turner. The two boys locked eyes, sizing each other up. Tommy was all about posturing as he inflated his chest, pulling his shoulders back. Turner's dark eyes had burned intensely as he responded to Tommy's not-so-subtle dominant male of the species display. There was menace in Turner's eyes.

"Are you a soccer player then?" Truly asked of Tommy. "You look like a striker if I had to venture a guess." She smiled at Tommy, and I was almost sure she batted her eyes at him. At this point, I would take any diversion to break up the tension. "So, do you like to score?" she asked.

Well, almost any diversion. Her last comment made me want to bang my head on the table—I was embarrassed enough for the both of us. Luckily, Tommy didn't appear to catch the double meaning.

"I do play striker, how did you know?" Tommy grabbed a chair, spinning it around and sat across from Truly. Arms folded across the chair back, he smiled at Truly, waiting for her answer.

This was my opportunity to further diffuse the ticking time bomb otherwise known as my life. "Can I talk to you?" I asked Turner, grabbing his arm, wanting to move him away from Tommy.

I started to stand and everything came to a screeching halt.

My plate. My peas. My breath caught in my throat as I looked down. The symbol was back, this time arranged on my plate using my untouched peas. What did it mean? I glanced toward Tommy and Renata, but they hadn't noticed. Truly was looking at me with an odd expression, no doubt considering the possibility I was having an aneurysm right there in the cafeteria.

Time to leave. Turner allowed himself to be led away as we made our way outside. When we paused under the large oak shading the entrance, he looked at me and said, "What was that about?"

"What was what about?" I could play dumb when I needed to. And I really needed to at that moment. My mind was still racing. I was clearly on the receiving end of a message, but I had absolutely no idea what it meant. The symbol didn't look at all familiar. Why would that particular symbol keep showing up when it didn't convey any meaning to me whatsoever?

And then there's the other half of the question: Who? Who was trying to communicate with me? I knew I wasn't normal. Ghosts, spirits, whatever you want to call them have always come to me, but never this way. Never so mysteriously.

"Abbey?" Turner looked at me with those eyes of his.

"Yes?"

"Are you all right? You looked as if you saw a ghost back there." His concern made me feel better.

"Did you see my plate?" Turner had a quizzical look, so I tried to clarify. "My peas, to be more precise."

"That's so much clearer. Thank you."

I took a deep breath. "For the last several days, a symbol has been appearing around me." Turner looked like he was going to ask something, but I didn't give him the chance. "It showed up on the wall of Charlotte's—Mrs. Bies'—office and faded from sight before our eyes. The next morning I saw the symbol traced onto my bed sheet. And just now, my peas were arranged into the same symbol. I don't know who—or what—is trying to communicate with me."

This was the part I hated. In the past when I've shared some of what goes on in my life, I didn't always get the response I was hoping for. Most of the time people don't believe me, or they think I was kidding. If I persist, the look becomes one of concern as they mentally question my sanity. To tell the truth, at that point I usually just let them off the hook. I'd smile and say I was kidding.

Quarterflash had a hit with "Harden my Heart." The part I remember is the chorus where they sang about swallowing tears and hardening their hearts. Where friends are concerned, that's exactly what I've learned to do. My past is littered with friends who didn't believe, friends I couldn't confide in and others I wished could have been a friend, but I just couldn't risk the hurt. I couldn't remember the last time I had a close friend.

Don't get me wrong. This wasn't a pity party. My life isn't a sad thing; actually it's quite the opposite. It never failed to give me a tingle that I could do something no one else could. And I am secure enough to realize my differences are worth celebrating. There was a bright side to my lack of friendships: it had brought me closer to my dad, which in turn had led to worldwide travels and adventure. Not a bad life for a 14-year-old girl from Minnesota.

Turner was staring at me. I knew the expression coloring his face. I'd seen it too many times.

"Peas? Really?" He glanced back at the entrance. "Hang on," he said and disappeared through the door, leaving me to wonder what he was up to.

In a moment, he was back. Turner's expression had changed, but I wasn't able to read him well enough to see where this was going. He held up his cell phone. On screen was a close up picture of my plate, the arranged peas evident. "And you didn't do this?"

I suspected he'd known the answer before he asked. My father would call it doing his due diligence. You have to rule out the most likely scenarios before you can consider the more extreme options.

I shook my head.

"Have odd things like this happened to you before you came here?"

I nodded. "Odd things yes. Odd things like these symbols, no."

"Give me an example, if you would."

Sigh. "When I was little, I often spent the weekend at my great grandmother's house with my cousin, Sally. We slept up in the attic bedroom: a large, spooky room where the wind howled at night. After dark when we were in bed, we'd try to sleep as we listened to the wind and the creaks all old houses seem to have. Most nights, a figure would emerge from the closet on the far wall, the darkest part of the room. It was always the same: an older woman dressed in flowing white stepped silently into the room. She had a gaunt face, a face that looked as if the tragedies of life had made their mark, leaving her bitter and resentful. This apparition pointed at us accusingly, a silent scream evident from her open-mouthed expression. I have to tell you, it was a horrifying sight to witness."

Turner touched me on the arm, a gentle gesture reassuring me far more than words ever could. "What did you do?"

"Sally would scream for my great grandmother. But you see, my great grandmother was an old school woman who didn't have the patience for the games little girls play. The first time this happened, she came running up the stairs, the sound of her wooden shoes sounding like hammer blows on the steps. Of course, there wasn't anything in the room when she got there. The old woman figure faded away as soon as my great grandmother hurried up the stairs."

I shook my head at the memory. "It's not like that was the first time I've seen something unusual. Sure, I was scared, but nowhere near as terrified as Sally was. I remember holding her, feeling her body shake with fear and adrenaline. It took her a long time to settle down. It happened the next night, just the same as the first. Only my great grandmother didn't come running. It was bad. Sally completely lost it and sort of went away for a while. She never visited there again. And her family moved to another state several months later."

Turner shook his head. "Intense. Do you believe this symbol is some sort of sign?"

I nodded. "Yes, but I don't have a clue what it means. If I'm supposed to do something based on the symbol, well, it's not going to happen until they give me something more to work with. I hope lives aren't hanging in the balance."

Turner held my gaze, as I wondered what he was thinking. His hesitation brought instant regret about my over-sharing. "I'm not sure if I can help with the paranormal stuff, but I will have your back. If that helps..."

I fought back my tears, unable to voice a response. All I could offer in return was a nod. Years of loneliness will do that to a girl.

I got the smoldering eyes again as he helped me to my feet. "I can't say I've ever met anyone quite like you, Abbey."

Doubt set in as I walked back to Grimm Hall. I desperately hoped Turner's remark was meant as a positive.

16
Ninja Turtles on Speed

A shocking discovery today.

Alone in my room, I was working through the day's events. Lying on my bed and staring at the ceiling, I pondered what it all meant like some long-dead Greek philosopher. And it wasn't the underlying meaning of life. It was that damned symbol—pardon my French. But I was seriously concerned my brain might explode if I didn't figure out the answer soon.

Frustrated, I rolled over and faced Stacia's half of the room, looking at her backpack. It took a moment, but then it hit me faster than a ninja turtle on speed. Off my bed, I crossed the room in a heartbeat pulling a blue sweater—the exact powder blue sweater Truly wore—out of Stacia's backpack.

Stunned, I was left with a big question: Were Stacia and Truly the same person?

Ms. Neuman waved me into her office. I wasn't exactly sure how I felt about being there after my last visit. Talking about my mother brought up a lot of feelings I'd hidden away for a long time. It still felt raw, talking about her again. I'd almost rather spend an hour discussing my life in the ghetto. Almost.

Taking my usual seat, we sat quietly, each of us enjoying the awkward silence. I found myself once again taking stock of what Ms. Neuman was wearing. Today, she had on a gray lace top, pinstriped slacks and gray and black snakeskin pumps. If nothing else, she's taught me the importance of accessorizing. As far as her counseling, it was like a shop teacher with missing fingers, you don't exactly trust the safety message.

Her eyes coolly studied me, no emotion evident. I think she was waiting for me to initiate the conversation. Well, I had some news for her. She was going to be waiting a long freakin' time.

Two long minutes later, I began to realize she was quite good at this. I fidgeted and looked around the room, as I couldn't hold her gaze. I studied the book titles, not finding anything interesting. Time moved slower and slower, the silence feeling impossibly loud. I couldn't take it. She won.

"So," I ventured.

Her eyebrow raised, but she held her silence. She was *really* good at this.

"What have you been up to?" I asked Ms. Neuman. "Been having a good summer?" I'd keep this light and impersonal. No more tears for me.

Leaning back and reaching for something, Ms. Neuman said, "What have I been up to? Funny thing you should ask. I was off campus last night and stopped by a bookstore. Barnes and Noble have a great selection of books. Their geography section is second to none." She had a book in her hands, which she handed to me.

Tentatively, I accepted the offered book. Turning it over, the title took my breath away: *The CIA's Guidebook to Venezuela*. The back cover copy read:

> *This authoritative book offers a comprehensive assessment of contemporary Venezuela. Highlighting the need to avoid simplistic assessments of the past and present, it offers a clear-eyed understanding of Venezuelan reality today. This groundbreaking book details the true story of the CIA and US Coast Guard's secret mission to overthrow the Venezuelan government to gain control of the country's oil. Also discussed are the dangers for both locals and outsiders in the notorious badlands of the Guajira Peninsula on the*

Venezuela-Colombia border. Chock full of the latest Google Earth images and on-the-ground accounts by CIA operatives, you will experience a Venezuela like few others have.

Interesting.

"I thought it would make sense for you to learn more about the land and people who meant so much to your mother. The book is yours to keep, Abbey. Let's cut our session short tonight so you can look through the book. We'll spend a little more time together tomorrow if that's all right with you."

Nodding, I let her escort me to the door and that was that.

WALKING BACK TO THE DORM, I debated what to do about Stacia and her fake sister, Truly. Not wanting to confront Stacia, and have her deny the Truly hoax, I needed a plan. A plan that would make it evident her hoax was just that. For now, it was better to keep my newfound knowledge to myself. And for some reason, it was comforting to know I wasn't the only strange one in camp.

I found myself wanting to talk to my mom again. "Hey, Mom. Hope you're doing great. Guess what? I just got a book on Venezuela. Surprisingly, I got it from my counselor. There may be more to her than I thought. I'm curious to learn about the country you loved so much. I just wish you had come back from there. Remember the Prince song I used to sing along with? Except now when I hear 'When Doves Cry,' it reminds me of you and I get sad. Please come back. I want to be able to sing along with Prince again."

17

ONE MYSTERY SOLVED...

I was a stalker.

As cat-like as possible, I'd been following Stacia around camp. Wherever she went, I was her shadow. It'd taken a day and a half before I witnessed Stacia going into the bathroom and moments later, Truly coming out.

It was funny that now that I looked for it, I realized Truly always wore the same oversized powder blue sweater. Her hair was worn in a casual up-do, while Stacia wore her hair down. Truly had glasses, while Stacia didn't—which I'm sure had just plain glass for lenses. Add the southern accent and Stacia was magically transformed into the far more intelligent girl from South Carolina, Truly.

This was a disguise worthy of Clark Kent. How Lois Lane never noticed the similarity was beyond me.

Watching my prey from around a pillar at the University Center, I almost blew my cover when a hand touched my shoulder. Expecting—and truth be told, hoping—it was Turner, I was surprised to find Mr. Kindle when I turned around.

"Miss Hill," he began a little too loud for my tastes.

Since Mr. Kindle was the man who yelled at me the last time we spoke, I was ready to give him a few things to think about. However, this wasn't the time or place to resume our previous argument—I just wanted him to go away. Quietly.

"About our discussion the other day, I have been giving it further consideration. I believe, as most enlightened Christians should, we must allow for the freedom of God to use people—both living and dead—for his good purposes. This is his world, after all. God set up the physical and moral laws and He rules over these in love. When something is needed for his children, He spares no expense." Slipping off his glasses, Mr. Kindle wiped them on a white handkerchief pulled from his breast pocket.

"Really?" I asked.

He smiled a fatherly smile. "Really. I happened to find a C.S. Lewis anecdote that was quite persuasive. Apparently, moments after his death at Cambridge, C.S. Lewis appeared in the Oxford bedroom of J.B. Phillips, a dear friend of his, the man who translated the Bible in the Phillips translation. At the time, Phillips was in a deep depression that threatened his life. He refused to leave his chambers, refused proper food or exercise, and seriously questioned the love and election of God in his life. A 'healthy Lewis, hearty and glowing' as Phillips was later to record, stood before him, entering his room through closed doors."

I took a quick glance around the pillar to find Stacia still talking with a group of girls.

Mr. Kindle paused as he wiped his glasses. "In this vision, Lewis spoke only one sentence to Phillips: 'J.B., it's not as hard as you think.' One solitary sentence, the meaning of which is debated to this day; however, what was not debated was the effect of that sentence. It snapped Phillips out of his depression and set him once again following God. After Lewis had spoken that cryptic sentence, he disappeared."

Now clean, Mr. Kindle slid his glasses back in place. "Phillips came out of his chambers only to find Lewis had died moments before the appearance, miles away. He pondered this in his heart with wonder, and never returned to his depression. Now, was this a case of God giving a soul a detour on the way to heaven to save a special friend? Who knows? The fact that this encounter with a spirit was such a redemptive one leads me to believe it's an authentic encounter. However, only God knows for sure."

I was confused by Mr. Kindle's sudden switch to being nice. However, over my many years, I've found adults had such a rigid hold on what their reality should be, it often became the catalyst sending them off the commonsense path. And my last encounter with a spittle spewing Mr. Kindle had him so far off the path he couldn't possibly see it from where he was.

Mr. Kindle turned to leave, but I had one more question for him. "Wait, how would I know if the spirit is from God or from somewhere else?" I was genuinely curious about his answer.

Gathering himself for his big exit, he looked me in the eye. "Well, Miss Hill, I guess it would come down to the motivation. Is there a redemptive quality to the encounter? Will someone be helped or saved by the interaction? I can't imagine God bending his physical and moral laws for anything less." With that, Mr. Kindle turned with a flourish and departed for greener pastures.

Mr. Kindle was a rock star. Just when I thought I had him figured out, *boom*! The man swooped in with a game changing new outlook. One of the reasons I took to my mother's love of Eighties music was the imagery the songs gave me. Take "Rock Me Amadeus," for example. The Falco song shed light on classical music composer Amadeus Mozart. Nobody thought he'd had a wild side, but there it was: wine, women and song.

Rock on, Amadeus—and Mr. Kindle.

BACK IN STALKER mode and with a plan of action, I carefully approached Stacia from behind, placing one foot in front of the other.

Ten feet.

Dropping my backpack, I switched my highlighter to my left hand.

Seven feet.

I removed the cap and slid the exposed point between my second and third fingers.

Five feet.

Stacia was on my left and I made a diagonal approach from behind her right shoulder.

Three feet away now.

Clueless, she hadn't yet caught on to my ninja-like stealthiness.

One foot away, I could reach out and touch her. Stacia wore a T-shirt and I grasped her arm just above the elbow.

"Hey, Stacia. What's going on?" I asked innocently. The highlighter made contact while I kept my hand on Stacia's elbow.

"We just found out we have a scavenger hunt coming up. It's supposed to be a really big deal. We're going to be split into teams and given several hours to complete the hunt. It's supposed to help us work together, but I have my doubts that'll happen, though." Stacia shook her head, a wry smile on her face.

Removing my hand from her arm, I switched the highlighter to my right hand, keeping it out of Stacia's view. The marker had done its job and there was a dime-sized green dot just above her elbow. "Sounds like fun. I haven't been on a scavenger hunt since Girl Scouts back in fourth grade."

"Knowing our camp staff, this is going to be a very different experience than a Girl Scout scavenger hunt," Renata said. "I'm guessing there'll be an element of danger involved. You know, alligator pits to cross, possibly automatic weapons fire to crawl underneath and certainly verbal abuse to keep us on our toes. A delightful experience for one and all."

"I just hope we live to tell about it," Stacia said.

"Me too," I replied. "The lawyers will need our testimony to lock up these guys and throw away the key." This got a laugh, but Stacia elbowed me as she jerked her head toward a nearby Mr. Johnson. His stern look was enough to get us moving toward the exit. I glanced over my shoulder and found Mr. Johnson watching us and we locked eyes for an instant. I can tell one thing for certain, there was no love in his gaze. I prayed he hadn't heard our conversation. I didn't want to get any further on Mr. Johnson's bad side, as I already had an enormous target painted on my back.

AFTER OUR GATHERING TIME, we headed back to Grimm Hall and I spotted a pale blue sweater up ahead. Knowing this was my moment, I sped up and closed the gap.

"Hey, Truly," I said touching her right shoulder. She turned around and I let a look of disgust cross my face as I jerked my arm away. "Oh gross."

"What?" she demanded. "What is it?"

"There's a big spider on the back of your sleeve. Gross," I said.

Truly had a moment of panic and frantically pulled off the sweater, shaking it to dislodge the spider. The thing was, there wasn't a spider.

There was, however, a green dot just above her elbow.

Gotcha.

18

DON'T QUIT YOUR DAY JOB TO BECOME A MOTIVATIONAL SPEAKER

The morning came way too early—and so did our physical training. Facing our über training instructor, Mr. Johnson wasn't the way I preferred to start my day.

The room buzzed with talk of the upcoming scavenger hunt. Speculation abounded. Mr. Johnson's entrance quieted the room as he held up his hand looking for our full attention. He glanced around the room, pausing at certain students. I was one of the lucky ones and his look spoke volumes as he stared at me. I was not and never will be one of his pets. I was okay with that. I didn't particularly care for him either.

"I want to take a moment to brief you on our upcoming scavenger hunt. This hunt will not be like others you might have had the pleasure of participating in. This will be a rigorous test of your mental and physical abilities. We will be assigning teams of four individuals to work together to complete a set of clues. If you do not function together, you will fail. If you do not use your brains, you will fail. And if you do not use your maximum physical abilities, you will fail."

He paused, looking around the room. I leaned over to Stacia. "He's a shining ray of sunshine, isn't he?" I whispered.

"If I were him, I wouldn't quit my day job to become a motivational speaker."

Just like sitting in church as a child, once I start to giggle, there was no stopping me. I tried to hide it, but I was unsuccessful and Mr. Johnson's gaze slid my way. Facing certain punishment, I started coughing.

"I need water," I gasped out between coughs. Turning away, I headed for the water fountain. I was still giggling as I leaned down to get a drink. With a supreme effort, I regained enough composure to rejoin the group.

I got a wary look from Mr. Johnson as he paused for a long moment. Me, I just offered my sweetest smile while I counted backward from 100 to keep my mind off further giggles. I got down to 84 before he gave up and returned to the other kids in the room.

"The scavenger hunt will take place next Friday. It will take the top teams at least two hours to complete the hunt, while those teams with underachievers," he said and I swear he made a point to look at me, "will be lucky to finish in less than four hours. Do you want to know what you're playing for?"

This is the part of *Survivor* where Jeff Probst, the host, tells the group what fabulous prize will be theirs when they outwit, outlast and outplay the other team. I liked this part, and the group sounded excited as he made them wait for the answer.

"Pride," he said, enjoying the disappointed groans around the room. This was the first moment I'd seen him smile without looking like a hyena ready to bite the legs off of a wounded animal. "The pride that comes from doing a job well. What better reward could there possibly be?"

Not waiting for our answer, Mr. Johnson continued, "Let's get to the morning fun. We'll start with plyometrics and finish with some good old-fashioned rope climbing. I hope you're ready to sweat."

There were groans all around. Trying to keep a positive attitude, I remembered the Billy Ocean song, "When the Going Gets Tough, the Tough Get Going." The song's energy gave me enough energy of my own to get through the morning's activities. I got a few funny looks as I was singing, but I didn't care. I was tough when I needed to be.

BACK IN MY ROOM, I paged through the book on Venezuela Ms. Neuman gave me. I was surprised by how different the various parts of the country were. The larger cities were modern while other parts of the country were virtually prehistoric. Reading about the life there, I picked up on the spirit of the people, the sort of spirit that would be attractive to my mother. There was exuberance for life there, allowing for a positive outlook despite less than ideal conditions. My mom was always a positive person and appreciated the same quality in others.

Having Colombia as a neighbor apparently had its challenges. The Colombian drug cartel's influence has damaged Venezuela in many ways. Besides the spread of drugs, kidnapping has been rampant. The cartels held people captive for ransom, asking for exorbitant sums of money—especially for such a poor country. It was an early theory that my mom was kidnapped, but no ransom was ever demanded. The book portrayed the tragedy of how many of Venezuela's youth were corrupted by the lure of the cartel's money. They left their families behind for a life of crime, violence and greed, forgetting the very values holding their families together in the first place.

Many of the Colombian drug processing facilities were located inside the insubstantial borders of Venezuela, which were basically jungles. There wasn't enough law enforcement to deter these criminal activities, meaning the cartels were free to do whatever they wanted in these compounds.

The chemicals used in the drug manufacturing process had hurt Venezuela's environment. They didn't have the controls that the US had; there wasn't an Environmental Protection Agency to monitor the process. Chemicals were dumped, infecting the ecosystem for miles around as well as much further downstream from the drug manufacturing facility. The effects could be quite devastating. The book detailed the recent account of a mass kill of amphibians traced to the spillage of chemicals used for drug processing. The actual spill had occurred miles upstream from where the kill had taken place.

"Hey," Stacia said as she jumped on my bed. "What are you doing?" She looked at the book cover in my hand. She gave me a little roll of her eyes, knowing where the book had come from.

"I thought I should at least look at it." I put the book down, looking at Stacia. "Maybe I am learning something here at camp. I'm realizing I can't duck and hide from who I am."

Crossing my legs, I leaned forward. "Sure, there have been injustices, so what? Life isn't always fair. But I need to focus on my present and start preparing for my future. I feel that's why I am here. This camp—despite its many faults—has changed me. I look at things differently, realizing I need to understand who I am and be willing to take on whatever life throws at me. I am not the same naïve girl who first arrived here."

Stacia was nodding. "I like it. You're kicking butt and taking names."

"Whatever that means."

Stacia grinned. "It means you went from princess to warrior."

"Exactly. I'm not avoiding the difficult situations—I'm meeting them head on. I remember a quote from the *Art of War*: If you know the enemy and know yourself, you need not fear the result of a hundred battles. From now on, that's how I roll."

I held up the book. "After my mom's disappearance, I tried not to think about her. It was too painful. I didn't want to hear about Venezuela or even South America. But that part of the world was important to my mother. And now, from reading about Venezuela, I can see the struggles they have to deal with every day. It sure puts my camp experience into perspective."

"I don't know anything about South America. What kind of struggles are we talking about?" Stacia asked.

"I was reading about the area of Venezuela bordering Colombia. The drug cartels are destroying not only the environment but the people's entire way of life. They recruit young people and make them soldiers of the cartel, so it's nearly impossible to stop them. And the chemicals used in the drug processing are dumped directly into the water with no concern for the harm it causes downstream. There was this mass kill of amphibians..."

"Amphibians? You mean like frogs?"

"Yeah, there were thousands killed..." I glanced at Stacia. Her expression was enough to connect my obviously slow brain synapses. "Oh, my..."

Stacia took the book and frantically paged through it until she paused and thrust it back at me. I was looking at a large picture of a marsh-like field. Photographed from a low angle, the picture showed a man kneeling by a metal pail. He wore mud-caked rubber boots, canvas shorts and a handkerchief pulled over his mouth and nose—presumably to help him deal with the stench. The stench arising from all the dead frogs surrounding him. There had to be thousands of them in the picture. Little white bellies motionless in the mud as far as the camera's eye could see.

What did it mean? Could it really be a coincidence that the oddest thing that's ever happened to me—and that's saying a lot—also happened in the same country where my mother disappeared?

"Do you believe in coincidences?" I asked Stacia. She shook her head, her eyes deer-in-the-headlights wide.

"Me neither."

19
FALLING COWS

I was waiting outside Ms. Neuman's office, trying to overhear her conversation with Amanda. Amanda was this perfect looking girl from the suburbs. She seemed nice enough, except for the fact that she liked to start fires. At least that was the rumor about her. Of course, you couldn't believe everything you heard around camp. Just to be on the safe side, I wasn't leaving any dry kindling lying around my room. A girl couldn't be too safe.

Muffled voices came from behind the closed door. Frustrated, I got up and moved closer—just as the door opened. Not wanting to get caught, I jumped back as Ms. Neuman gestured for Amanda to go first. Amanda may have suspected I was eavesdropping as she gave me the stink eye. Not wanting to sink to her level, I just stuck out my tongue at her. I got the desired reaction, her mouth wide open.

"Come on in, Abbey," Ms. Neuman said, oblivious to Amanda's juvenile behavior.

I took my customary spot across from her, tucking my legs underneath. I looked at Ms. Neuman, letting her speak first. After all, it was her agenda, not mine.

"Have you had an opportunity to look through the book I gave you?"

I nodded.

"How did it make you feel? Since your mother loved the country so fondly, were you able to see what captivated her about the Venezuelan people?"

I'd already decided I wasn't going to mention my discovery. No good could come from raising those issues. "Well," I began, "it was interesting to read about the people my mom cared for. I can see what led her to return to Venezuela time after time. She loved the spirit of the people there. Despite all the challenges they face, their positive attitude never quits."

Ms. Neuman nodded. "I see. Let me ask you a question. After your mom disappeared and you realized she wouldn't be coming back, did you quit? Did you give up on being her daughter and having her as your mother? Did you push away your memories of her?" She tucked a stray strand of hair behind her ear and leaned in close. "And didn't it leave a hole in your heart—one that just happens to be shaped in your mother's image?"

I was crying now. I couldn't help it.

"But it was so sudden, there was no warning. She was just ripped away from us..." There weren't any more words, only sobs.

Getting up from her chair, Ms. Neuman knelt in front of me. "Abbey, I am sorry. It's always that way. Things happen when you're not expecting them." She stood and removed a newspaper article pinned to her bulletin board. "I've kept this article as a reminder," she said, handing it to me.

The headline read:

FALLING COW CRUSHES CAR

Intrigued, I read on.

The Strunk family was on a family trip through the Oregon hills when the unlikely happened. A large cow fell from an overlooking cliff and totaled their car. A Chelan County fire chief said the family was lucky, missing being killed by a matter of inches. The 600-pound cow fell about 200 feet and landed on the hood of the Strunk's new Chrysler Pacifica. The fire chief believes the cow had fallen from a ledge overlooking the winding highway. No one was injured; however, the cow—and the Pacifica—were both beyond repair. "I had no idea what had happened until it was over. We got out of the car, completely dazed, and found this very large cow lying across the hood of my new car," Charles Strunk commented.

I looked up at Ms. Neuman, not getting the relevance. She said, "The thing is, Abbey, there will always be falling cows. Life isn't always going to be smooth and predictable. In your life, cows will drop. You won't see them coming, and you won't know what happened until it's over. The only thing you can do is accept it and roll with whatever life throws your way—or drops on you. Having the ability to cope and change directions at a moment's notice might just be the thing that keeps you alive."

Walking out of the Wyman entrance, I couldn't help but stop and scan the skies. Falling cows. I couldn't say anyone had warned me about them before.

"Hey, mom. Hope the weather is good where you're at," I said out loud as I walked back to the dorm. "Remember that Eighties power ballad 'Every Rose Has Its Thorn?' We'd be singing along and Dad would giggle as we hammed it up for him. It's the meaning behind the song that's sticking with me: that for every good in life, there's a bad too. It's like when you traveled to all those other countries. For all the good you did by going to Venezuela to help the poor with their medical needs, I would miss you terribly for the weeks you were gone. But, then to have you not come back...well, that's the biggest thorn of them all." As it often did in moments like this, my eyes threatened to leak. I wiped the corners of my eyes and quickened my pace.

Boom. Boom. Boom. Boom. Boom.
My heart racing, I lurched up in bed, startled out of my sleep by

the heavy pounding on our door. I had no idea what time it was, but I knew it was the middle of the night. Stacia was asleep on her bed across the room. How could she not have heard the pounding?

My heart was hammering. The thing was, no one pounds on your door in the middle of the night with good news. I couldn't ignore the door, so I slid out of bed and crept over to it. I paused with my hand on the knob. Stacia was still asleep, her breathing slow and regular. Afraid the pounding would resume, I ever so slowly pulled the door open.

This was the part I hate in scary movies. You know something was out there, waiting for the victim—usually an unwitting teenage girl, much like myself—to step out. And they always did, leaving their position of safety to satisfy their curiosity. By all reports, it wasn't just cats that have suffered for their curiosity. People died too. Yet I stepped out from behind the door. I've never been one to ignore the unknown.

Empty. There wasn't anyone out in the hall. Heavy pounding like I heard should have woken up everyone on this floor, yet mine was the only open door.

Down the hall, I caught movement in the corner of my eye. The bathroom door was swinging shut. I needed answers and the best option for getting them just went into the bathroom. Barefoot, wearing only boxers and a T-shirt, I made my way down the hall.

At the bathroom door, I took a deep breath and pushed it open. The lights were off and my fingers slid along the wall searching for the switch. Finding it, I flipped it on, firing up the ancient fluorescent lights mounted to the ceiling. The lights crackled and flickered, sporadically sending out harsh blue light followed by shadows. The effect was like walking into a room lit by a single strobe light at the state fair haunted house.

The air was heavy with moisture, the mirrors fogged over. Given our early morning physical training, I couldn't imagine anyone up in the middle of the night taking a long shower—in the dark. Looking around the room in the flickering light, it was clear I was the only one there. I turned to leave and...

The line was drawn in slow motion, moving from top to bottom. It was as if a finger touched the fogged mirror and drew the symbol that's been plaguing me since I got to camp. The unseen finger had finished the curved vertical line and begun adding the horizontal line, moving left to right. After a moment, it was followed by a dot just off to the bottom right of the symbol. I could almost see the finger moving in a circle to create the dot. I was frozen in place staring at the mysterious symbol, as condensation ran down the mirror.

The eerie flickering strobe effect of the light suddenly ended, the bathroom bathed in cold blue light. I couldn't help but shiver as something caught my eye and stopped me in my tracks.

The symbol was now on each of the eight mirrors in the room.

20
TROUBLE WITH TURNER

I was being pulled in way too many directions.

I felt like the daycare teacher at snack time, with two-dozen sticky little hands pulling on you to get your attention. First, there was Turner, with his long dark hair covering those amazing eyes of his. Second, there was this camp I was trying to survive with its mean staff and grueling physical challenges. And then there was this mysterious symbol that kept showing up. I had this nagging feeling if I could get Turner off my mind for a while, I'd be able to figure out the mystery behind the symbol.

It was a tough morning of plyometrics—if I had to do jump squats ever again, it would be too soon—but at least they played Van Halen's classic, "Jump." *Might as well jump*, I thought, as we did still another set.

Afterward, I met up with Turner. Soaked with sweat, his T-shirt clung to his ripped abs, demanding my attention. Turner's amused expression suggests he'd noticed my attention. We walked down to the Kinnickinnic River and plopped down by the riverbank. He leaned back, fingers clasped behind his head and I did the same. It felt good to let the morning sun warm my tired body.

"Why are you here?" I asked, wanting to know what transgression landed Turner in this prison camp. So far, he hadn't shared anything about himself. A complete vault. Better than the alternative—Tommy, for instance, whose favorite topic was Tommy.

Turner rose up onto an elbow. "Why am I here? Because you asked if I wanted to go for a walk. You may have a good memory, but it's a bit short." I got his grin.

"Funny. Tell me how you ended up spending your summer vacation here. Was it your idea?"

Shaking his head, Turner smiled. "Hardly. I have my doubts anyone would knowingly volunteer for this abuse. I wasn't exactly keen on the idea as you might imagine, but my father insisted." Turner let out a big sigh. "My father—the former marine—said I lacked discipline. Discipline. How many 15-year-old kids do you know that are disciplined? Exactly. It's not like I was out stealing cars or robbing Quick-E-Marts."

"Or rustling horses," I offered.

"Or rustling horses." From the look on Turner's face, I'd completely derailed his train of thought.

"It was never bad things," he said after a moment.

"Wait, what do you mean?" So there was a reason beyond strict parenting.

"I never tried to do anything mean or illegal."

"Turner, what did you do?"

"Nothing really." But he looked guilty. If he'd been a cat, I wouldn't even have to look to know the canary was dinner. Turner wouldn't look at me.

"Turner, spill. What did you do?" I let some exasperation creep into my voice.

"It was just a few pranks."

I felt some relief. This could have been so much worse. "Pranks?"

Turner nodded.

"Like what? Give me an example." I folded my arms trying to look stubborn.

Looking down, he spoke softly, "I placed a fake ad on Craigslist claiming Robert Salisbury of Medina, Minnesota had abandoned his property and the Hennepin County Sheriff's Department was authorizing people to take away his belongings for free, including his horse. From what I gather, the only reason Salisbury came home to anything left in his house, was because a woman called him before she took his horse. She was worried about what to feed it. I guess

Salisbury raced home to find at least 30 people rummaging through his house and his barn, loading his possessions into their cars and trucks and all of them refusing to give the stuff back. When he protested, claiming his stuff was not abandoned, people waved printouts of the Craigslist advertisement. They said this proved they were in the right to take his stuff. They honestly believed just because it appeared on the internet, it was true. It boggles the mind."

OMG. I looked at Turner absolutely astounded. "Are you nuts? You look like a normal, high-functioning member of society. But no... Whatever made you think that was a good idea?"

Turner simply shrugged, so I pressed for more information. "Did you even know the guy, Salisbury?"

Still not holding my eyes, Turner said, "Salisbury was our school principal."

This made me fall right back into the grass. I couldn't help it. All I could do was laugh. It took a few long moments to regain my composure. "Why? What did he ever do to you?"

"Well, he did suspend me. Twice." There was that guilty look again.

"Umm...you don't get suspended for doing nothing." I sat up. "Turner, why were you suspended?"

"Which time?"

I rolled my eyes at him. "Why don't you start with the most recent time?"

"I went into a deserted classroom and got into the ceiling. It was simple from there. I stripped the wiring from the speaker system, hooked up an amplifier and made my own school announcement. It was a beautiful spring day, after all."

"What was your announcement?"

Turner had a silly grin on his face. "I said due to a break in the water main, school was canceled for the rest of the day."

I looked at Turner in a whole new light. "You are seriously deranged, you know that?"

He nodded. He knew.

"I hate to ask, but what was your other suspension for?" But I really did want to ask.

He had that grin again. "I just wanted to show some school spirit. What could be wrong with that? I went to East Middle School in Plymouth. Our big rival was West Middle School in Wayzata. Every year they always beat us in football. We played them twice each season and the first time they had killed us at home—the score was something like 37 - 3. Now we were going to play them in their Homecoming game. What better time to pull a little prank?" He looked at me for some encouragement or possibly validation. I just gave him a casual nod, which was enough to keep him talking.

"It took a lot of planning, a lot of late nights, however when you're working toward a goal, it's no big deal."

I interrupted. "Have you tried using your powers for good, instead of evil?"

"Funny." Turner gazed at the clouds and continued. "I scouted out their stadium and made a grid of the main four sections directly across from the visitor's seats. I printed up a mess of signs in black and white, each one tied to a specific seat. The signs said the school boosters want to honor the coach and for everyone to hold up their signs at the beginning of the third quarter. What they didn't realize was, when held up together the signs actually spelled out, 'West Sucks.' I had warned my friends to have their cameras ready to capture the event for YouTube. I probably went a bit too far notifying the scoreboard camera operator so he could film the coach's tribute. I believe it may have been my crowning achievement of middle school to see *West Sucks* up there on their fancy new scoreboard.

"Salisbury somehow learned I was behind the prank and called me to his office. He chewed me out for being mean-spirited and for showing unsportsmanlike behavior. Even as he yelled at me, I thought I detected a twinkle in his eye. Maybe unofficially, he'd enjoyed the prank. I got a three-day vacation for that one."

I had to smile. "That was pretty clever. How does one get started with pranks?"

"It began with telemarketers at first. They always called at the most inopportune times, at dinner or early Saturday mornings when I was trying to sleep. I decided to have some fun at their expense and was answering yes to every question, whether or not it was a yes or no question. They would eventually catch on and hang up. Sometimes I would put on my best Middle Eastern accent and ask them totally inappropriate things about their personal lives. Other times, I would flirt shamelessly, hitting on whoever happened to be on the phone—it didn't make a difference if it was male or female. The more awkward, the better. I lived to torment those people."

I was laughing. "I will be staying on your good side. You can be quite dangerous." As I held his eyes, the mood changed. I could feel the shift, as we both grew quiet, my pulse quickening, and his dark eyes reached right into my soul. Turner leaned into my space.

"Hey, let's go," a voice called out to ruin the moment. "Camp meeting."

Really? It would have been perfect, so perfect.

21

MAYBE THEY FOUND OUT ABOUT THE TOILET THING

I was standing in front of a firing squad.

My knees trembled and my heart pounded in my chest as they stared at me. I hope they would hurry and get it over with. We were gathered at the fire pit area, with the camp staff standing in front of us.

Maybe not a firing squad, but it felt very "us versus them." As we waited for the meeting to begin, there was plenty of whispering as everyone speculated about the reason for the meeting.

"Maybe the scavenger hunt is canceled."

"I bet they want to apologize for being so mean to us."

"Maybe they found out about the toilet thing."

"What if they want us to stay longer? I can't miss school."

"Suppose they got word the mothership was coming back for the counselors?"

"I swear I only took one. Okay, maybe it was two. But no more than four."

"We're being forced to join the glee club. I knew this place sucked."

"When's lunch?"

"It's the ghost thing." I swear the girl glanced in my direction as she said this. I looked away.

The same dour-faced man who wouldn't help me escape from the camp held up his hand. The whispering quickly quieted. His face had no expression whatsoever. This was a man who wouldn't smile even when the lottery official was handing him the oversized check in front of the cameras during the obligatory press conference. This man had no joy in his heart—clearly, he wasn't a breastfed baby, as my father would say.

"Our annual scavenger hunt starts after dinner tonight. We've broken you into teams of four. And no, there will be no switching players between teams. We have eight teams competing." He paused, looking around the group before giving a slight nod toward the camp staff. "We have decided to offer a little incentive this year. The top four teams will be allowed to miss physical training next week. However, the bottom four will be doing two-a-day physical training sessions all week long."

There was a unison groan echoing my sentiment at the prospect of seeing Mr. Johnson two times each day for a week straight.

"Trust me, you do not want to be in the bottom four. The workouts will be particularly difficult." Oddly enough, there was almost a hint of a smile there. Figured.

The staff spread out, each with a sheet of paper in hand. Mr. Johnson went first, "When you hear your name, come join your teammates and strategize a bit. You have to work together as a team to achieve your goal. However, you will not be able to see your first clue until the start of the competition tonight." He nodded to one of the staff members.

A counselor held up his sheet of paper and began to read. "Corey Palmer, Renata Anderson, Salina Prescott and Makao Day." The four tentatively moved towards the counselor, unsure what to do next.

Mr. Johnson was next. He read his four names, butchering the pronunciation of three out of the four names. I suspected he was doing it intentionally, as most people would have little difficulty with "Smith." He pronounced it as "Smitts."

I still hadn't heard my name as Charlotte read her list. I glanced over at Stacia and she just shrugged.

Mr. Kindle took his time reading the names off his list, over-enunciating each name. Mine was not one of them.

An older counselor I'd never met read her list. She put on her reading glasses after pushing the list away as far as her arms would reach. There was a snicker off to my left. My name wasn't on her list either. Three more teams to go.

The next two counselors read their list of names. I kept waiting to hear mine as the crowd shrunk to a handful. I glanced around to find Carrie was also waiting. I closed my eyes and repeated in my head, "Please, not Carrie, anyone else, but not Carrie."

When the counselors were finished, it was only Ms. Neuman left holding her list. Carrie was still waiting, too. Wonderful. Next to me was Stacia, thankfully. That made three so far. Who was the final person on our team? Looking behind me, I realized it was Turner. He caught me looking and smiled at me. Once again, we were thrown together.

Ms. Neuman glanced around. "No need to read my list. Come on up, guys."

There are times in life when you start seeing patterns emerge. Circumstances didn't seem so circumstantial when they were repeated time and time again. The same people seemed to turn up again and again. Could it really be a coincidence? Maybe we were part of a larger plan and for good or bad, certain people were placed in our path. If that was true, I wish the plan had been shared with me first. Was it too much to ask for a little control of my own life?

I glanced over at Carrie. She looked back at me. No emotion crossed her face. As a realist, I might not like Carrie, but her athletic ability could only help our team. Stacia was on the other end of the scale: not tall, slight build, no real muscle to speak of. But, she was whip-smart. If there was a puzzle to be figured out, she'd be the one I want on my team. Turner was an excellent addition as well. I realize my judgment might be a bit swayed where Turner was concerned, but his strength could really help us. As he charged through the obstacles, I will be right behind him.

"What's to strategize?" Stacia asked. "We won't know anything until we get the clues. Maybe then we could split up and get through the list in half the time."

Ms. Neuman shook her head. "You're missing the point. We want you to work together. This exercise is designed to have players work together for a common goal. So put it this way, splitting up will disqualify you and guarantee you a spot in the bottom four." She looked at each of us, holding our eyes for a long moment, the challenge evident in her dark eyes. "Anyone want to volunteer for two-a-day physical training workouts?"

None of us said a word. Clearly, we didn't have to.

"Good luck tonight," Ms. Neuman said with a long pause before she turned and walked away. I had the distinct feeling she wanted to add, "You'll need it."

My dad had a phrase he liked to use when one of us was facing a challenge. I remember once when my mom was worried about heading to a difficult part of the world, my dad said, "Eye of the tiger, Katherine." In our family, it meant you shouldn't have fear and go for it with everything you have. Clearly, my Mom's love of Eighties music had gotten to him too. Survivor's "Eye of the Tiger" lyrics were about rising to the challenge and going the distance.

Eye of the tiger, Abbey. Eye of the tiger.

22

ALL THE WORLD'S A STAGE

My heart pounded as we raced towards our first destination in the scavenger hunt. The whole thing felt out of control. First, they changed the rules on us. Every scavenger hunt I'd ever been on, we were given a list of items to gather. Sure, it was at Brittany's 8th birthday party, but my partner Eva and I were the winners. We totally crushed the other girls. Ahh, good times.

For this scavenger hunt, each team was handed a rolled up scroll of paper and instead of a list, we found a single clue. Each clue we solved would lead us to the next one. Apparently, we would use our physical prowess as well as mental abilities—though the first clue was totally obvious.

> *As a matter of course*
> *Just remember that before you slide*
> *This place can be a climb for some,*
> *But not an obstacle for others.*

The clue could only be referring to one place. When Turner read the clue out loud, we all shouted in unison, "The obstacle course." You have to climb the wall to get up to the platform—just before you slide down.

The second thing leaving me feeling out of control was Carrie, who wasn't exactly the ideal team player. After reading the clue, she sprinted for the course, leaving us behind. After a moment's hesitation, Turner took off after her. Stacia and I looked at each other, shrugged and sprinted after them. Way to be a team.

The sweat soaked through my T-shirt as I made my way up the hill, pulling Stacia along with me. The summer heat had lasted well into the evening. The air was thick and muggy, with the temperature hovering around 90 degrees. This time of year, the heat and moisture charged the atmosphere with enough energy to bring in some spectacular thunderstorms and even the occasional tornado. The sky was a bit hazy, but I didn't spot any threatening clouds on the horizon —which was good considering my fear of storms.

Carrie arrived at the obstacle course and dived for the tunnel after making quick work of the tires. Me, I was too busy laughing as we weren't running the obstacle course, just picking up the clue.

All three of us stood by the tunnel's exit as Carrie poked her head out. "Having fun?" Turner asked her, a smile on his face. "Let's focus on the job. You can always come back and finish the course on your own time." Carrie obviously did not like being teased, as she communicated her rebuttal with a single finger.

Stacia was already three-quarters the way up to the platform when we turned around. "So, we'll just wait down here, then?" I called up to her.

"Uh, huh." And she climbed onto the platform, moving out of sight.

It didn't take her long as Stacia let out a loud whoop and launched herself down the slide. She ended up sprawled out in the sand at the bottom, the scroll held tightly in her raised fist. "Yeah, baby," she said, the joy evident in her voice.

I plucked the scroll from her hand and slid off the light blue ribbon. The others crowded around to read the second clue.

> *The Kinnickinnic River is fun to say,*
> *As well as a great place to stay.*
> *If I gave up poetry to be an actor,*
> *This is where I would like to play.*

"The river." Turner pointed toward the nearby river.

Carrie grabbed his hand and redirected it. "Not so fast," she said. "They mean the Kinnickinnic River Theater."

"Carrie's right." I couldn't believe those words came out of my mouth. "The clue also mentions being an actor."

Stacia joined in. "And being in a play."

"Of course," Turner said. "Though I want to go on record right now, the clue writer should give up the poetry gig. For me, a poem that isn't classically structured is a complete waste of our time. The verses fall short of conveying the powerful imagery and emotion that can be truly transformational."

We all stopped and looked at Turner. Stacia had her mouth hanging open, while Carrie gave Turner the lovesick puppy look most teenage girls reserved for the picture of Justin Bieber cut out of Seventeen magazine and taped to their bathroom mirror. Gag me with a spoon.

"Hold on," I said, smelling something fishy. "Turner, I had no idea you were such an expert in literature. What exactly do you mean when you say a poem is classically structured?"

Turner had the look of sheepish embarrassment I see when I catch my father with a gas problem. "You know," he offered.

I wasn't letting him off the hook. "Pretend I know nothing about poetry. Pretend I'm not familiar with rhyming patterns, meter, grammar and imagery. I know nothing of how linguistic and intentional structures function in counterpoint to the metrical and stanzaic structures to create something far greater than the sum of its words. C'mon, humor me, Turner."

Shaking his head, Turner mumbled something incoherent.

"Pardon me?" I asked.

Turner looked me in the eye, regaining some of his usual swagger. "You can't trust any poem that doesn't begin with 'Roses are red; violets are blue.' I'm right, aren't I?"

I burst out laughing and the other two joined in. "You are such an idiot," I said shaking my head.

"Maybe. But you have to admit I'm the nicest idiot you know."

This time, it was easy to admit: he was right.

THE UNIVERSITY CENTER WAS DESERTED. Everyone must be involved in the scavenger hunt. As if to prove my theory, another group raced past, no doubt chasing down a clue. I heard a whoop of laughter as they rounded the corner at the end of the street.

"In the Air Tonight" by Phil Collins was classic Eighties. Opening with especially haunting drumbeats and guitar, the song captured the mood of impending drama. Oh, and there was also the greatest drum fill in history at roughly the halfway point. The crackle of thunder rippled across the summer sky and I shuddered. The storm was coming. It was in the air tonight.

Once inside, we took the stairs two at a time and reached the Kinnickinnic River Theater in a few moments. Outside, I was sweating like crazy as the air was thick with humidity. Inside, the air conditioning was cranked up so high, I was shivering. Somewhere in the middle of those two extremes would be nice.

Stacia was staring at me, and it took a moment before I caught on to her unspoken fear. Confidently, I grabbed a hold of her hand and whispered that it'll be fine, there were no more moving seats. Carrie and Turner followed us into the dimly lit theater.

A single overhead spotlight illuminated a circular portion of the stage no larger than a hula-hoop. Clearly, this was the spot. We took the stage as a group, as Stacia and I warily glanced around. Fortunately, not even a single chair was acting out of line. At the lighted circle—expecting to find another rolled up scroll in the center of the circle—I was perplexed when it wasn't there.

"Okay," Turner voiced our concern, "where's our clue?" He turned in place looking around.

"It has to be here somewhere. Let's spread out," Carrie said and headed to stage right, and Stacia shrugged, turning toward the other end of the stage. I headed for the darkness of the backstage area looking for a clue, feeling oddly like one of the girls in a Scooby Doo episode. Oh well, time to get jinky with it.

The overhead spot gave just enough light to make out indistinct shapes floating into my field of vision as I moved further into the dark. I hoped I could avoid running into sharp objects as I made my way further into the gloom. Just to be safe, I shuffled along with my arms outstretched looking like one of those bad movie zombies. Soon, a distant glow caught my attention. The neon green light was so diffused; it looked as if I was looking at it through a dense fog. As I got closer, the shape began to coalesce.

I felt the hair on the back of my neck stand up one by one as my brain made sense of what was in front of me. It was the symbol again.

The symbol's day-glow color looked like it was freshly painted— the green paint still running down the rough brick wall. I was fairly sure this paint wasn't available at my local Home Depot. I stared at the mark for a long minute, feeling helpless. I had no idea what it meant.

I heard Turner, some twenty yards behind me. He spoke in a loud, over-the-top theatrical style voice.

> *"All the world's a stage, and all the men*
> *and women merely players: they have*
> *their exits and their entrances; and one*
> *man in his time plays many parts,*
> *his acts being seven ages."*

I make my way onto the stage just as Turner finished, thrusting his hand up in dramatic fashion, as he stood in the lighted circle. I broke out into spontaneous applause as I heard Stacia give a loud whistle, her fingers in the corners of her mouth.

With a loud click, an overhead projector was brought to life. Rather than facing the stage for the audience to see, the projected screen had lit up the back wall, clearly meant for the stage actor's view only. And just like that, we had our next clue.

> *Some may ask, "Why boy?"*
> *However in a decade's time,*
> *The question will change,*
> *The answer just simple steps before you enter.*

23

FLASHES OF LIGNTING, ROLLS OF THUNDER

"You just needed to be an actor on stage, reciting lines from a Rodgers and Hammerstein musical," Stacia said as we gathered around looking at the words projected on the back wall.

"Umm, that was actually Shakespeare," Turner said uncomfortably.

"I didn't know he wrote musicals," Stacia responded with a twinkle in her eye. "What do you suppose our clue means?" she asked, looking back up at the enigmatic verses.

"Why boy?" Carrie said this out loud as she shifted her weight from side to side. "Why boy?"

"Why ask why?" Turner said to no one in particular.

The projector picked this moment to go black, the words fading into the wall.

After a moment's hesitation, we made our way up the aisle, anxious to get out of the theater. "Why boy?" Carrie said again.

"How would the question change after a decade?" Stacia asked.

"Good question," I offered.

"Thank you," she replied. "A decade is ten years. What happens after ten years to a boy?"

We all looked to Turner as we made our way down the steps into the University Center lobby. Another group was leaving out the front entrance. "Well?" Carrie asked Turner.

He held up his palms, shrugging. "He gets taller, stronger. His voice gets lower. Hair grows in funny places."

I elbowed Turner. "Most of that happens to a girl as well, you know. Maybe not the voice thing." We stepped out into the humid air as a nearby rumble of thunder suggested threatening weather was fast approaching.

"Our clue writer clearly makes the distinction it's a boy we are discussing. What else happens to a boy after ten years?"

Turner hesitated. "I don't know...he just becomes a man, I guess." Smiling, he flexed his bicep. I liked it.

"Why boy?" Carrie repeated. "Why man? Why man?"

"The Wyman Education Building!" I yelled, unable to keep cool. "It has to mean the Wyman building."

"That has to be it," Stacia agreed. "What else did the clue say?"

"Just simple steps before you can enter."

Obvious. We headed down the sidewalk at a run, feeling the urgency as a flash of lightning crackled overhead. The Wyman building was directly across a large grass courtyard from the University Center. However, after our experience with the squishy dead frogs, we stuck to the sidewalk.

Within a few minutes, we were at the steps. Sticking out of the wrought iron handrail was another rolled up scroll. It was in my hands before the others could grab it and I slid the blue ribbon off and uncurled the stiff parchment.

> It's not a darker hall,
> nor a hall filled with spiders,
> yet for Peter, it will echo,
> "Two, two, two."

This time, the clue wasn't so obvious. We huddled as another flash of lightning crackled overhead. Another shudder.

"This one is tougher," I offered.

"I don't get it." Carrie frowned.

"Me neither," Stacia added. She was the one I was counting on for the puzzles. She tried to redeem herself, though. "Let's break it down. Not a darker hall. A light hall then?"

"There are a lot of halls here. The buildings are full of them."
Carrie was clearly a master of the obvious.

"You know," Stacia said, "A lot of the buildings are named,
'Something Hall.' Maybe the clue is pointing to a particular hall."

"Peter Hall?" Carrie again.

"There's no Peter Hall," Turner said and then started laughing.

"What?" I demanded.

"I know where the clue is, c'mon." Heading back in the direction
we'd just come from, we looked to Turner for an explanation. He
kept us waiting. "This way," was all we got as we continued on Wild
Rose Avenue past the University Center.

Flashes of lightning, rolls of thunder. The sky came alive as the
last of the daylight crept out of sight. I glanced at my nonexistent
watch. It wasn't that late, was it? It should be light for another hour
this time of year. A fleeting glimpse told me the mass of dark storm
clouds centered over the campus was responsible for the gathering
darkness. An omen? I don't believe in omens. However, it couldn't
hurt to exercise some caution. You never know when a cow may be
dropping your way.

We made our way past the deserted Rodli Hall building, another
of the campus buildings under construction. Dark shapes inside the
windows manifested themselves as threatening figures to my
hyperactive imagination. I clearly had been under too much stress for
way too long. The physical and mental challenges had been taking
their toll on me. Next summer, no camp for me—it's Disney or
nothing.

We passed our home, Grimm Hall. It didn't feel like home, but it
was the closest thing I had here. "Heaven is a Place on Earth,"
another one of my go-to Eighties songs, was about hope and how we
have the ability to make our own heaven wherever we are. Any place
I could consistently lay my head down wasn't exactly a bad place.

Turner steered us toward the entrance of Parker Hall, the next
building we came to. "Parker Hall?" I asked.

"Yeah, Parker Hall," he replied. "You may not realize it, but I'm a closet geek."

"Oh, we realize it," Stacia said with a grin. She was always ready to dish it out.

Turner ignored her. "I've collected comic books since I learned to read. Spiderman has always been my favorite. I could identify with the nerdy teenager," he paused, looking at Stacia. "Nothing out of you."

Stacia simply held up her hands, palms out.

"That nerdy teenager was bitten by a radioactive spider. His name was Peter Parker." He paused, waiting for us to catch on. We looked at each other blankly.

"You don't get it? The clue mentions a darker hall, which rhymes with Parker Hall. It also mentions Peter and spiders. Obvious, right?"

"Obvious—if you're a geek," Stacia said holding up her hands. "Hey, you said it first."

"What are we waiting for? Let's go." I said, moving toward the entrance.

"Where to?" Carrie asked, still standing in place.

"Room 222," I said. "The final part of the clue."

Upstairs, we gently eased open the door—222 was stenciled on the old wooden door—as the door creaked open in protest. There was a creepy feeling about the place, and it wasn't just me. No one wanted to be the first to enter. But the thing was, we needed the clue, so I warily stepped into the room.

Completely deserted, the room didn't have a single piece of furniture on the floor and not a single picture hanging on the wall. Gray carpeting, gray walls. Seriously, this place needed to be on *Pimp my Dorm Room*. Where are the reality TV people when you needed them? The sparseness did have one benefit though: it was obvious the clue wasn't there.

"Nothing here," I said to my three teammates waiting at the door. They decided to join me and pushed into the room. We were all back-to-back, facing different directions looking for the clue. I didn't see it.

"Are you sure we're in the right place?" Carrie said, as she leveled a condescending look at Turner, "Maybe you should have spent more time reading real books."

I looked to Turner, who had that incredulous "you're throwing me under the bus after all I've done" look. His eyes burned a hole in Carrie and I sensed the anger rising in him.

"A real book? Like what, *Twilight? The Sisterhood of the Traveling Pants?* Please."

Carrie took a step closer toward Turner. "I read only non-fiction. Why give up the opportunity to learn real things from real people? Besides," she paused, "everyone knows Wonder Woman could take Spiderman in a fair fight."

We shifted our gaze waiting for Turner's response. He didn't keep us waiting. "You know, the last time I saw a woman in boots, wearing short shorts and carrying a magic lasso, she was being arrested in downtown Minneapolis for prostitution."

Turner stepped into Carrie's space, puffing out his chest. For the life of me, I couldn't tell if he was angry or having fun at Carrie's expense. Either way, I was good with it.

"And you honestly can't see a benefit from reading a book that sprung from someone's imagination? To boldly go where no one has gone before?" Turner asked. "Even Einstein said logic can take you from point A to point B, while imagination can take you anywhere."

Wanting to get us back on track, I hooked my arm in his and pulled him toward the door. "Come on, Captain Kirk. We need to rise above this argument." I paused, glancing above the door.

And there it was, hidden in a decorative tangle of vines, dried berries and stems. A rolled up scroll of paper tied with a baby blue ribbon. "The wall hanging," I said, pointing.

Turner reached for it, plucking our clue from its hiding place. I couldn't wait to see where this one would take us.

24

FAR FROM THE EDGE

If your fear is one of heights,
Or burns on your hands,
You may never reach the clue you seek.
There is one hope for you, and his name is Jim.

Things were looking up. An easy clue for a change. "Gonna be climbing some rope in the gym," I said. "My favorite."

"Mine too," Stacia said with a grin. "I enjoy having my shoulders pulled from their sockets." Stacia stepped out into the hallway after waving Carrie to go first. "On the plus side, we are getting closer to being done with this scavenger hunt."

"Good thing, the weather is looking dangerous out there."

The door was mostly glass and the lightning outside was near constant, one bright flash being overlapped by the next, looking every bit like a paparazzi-stalked Taylor Swift appearance.

I don't like storms.

Ever since I was a little girl, storms have terrified me. If there were even a slight chance of severe weather, I was paralyzed by my fear of what might happen—I wouldn't want to go anywhere. And whenever a storm threatened, I'd be glued to the weather channel, too afraid to do anything else. My fear got so bad, first thing each morning I looked at the day's forecast and checked the weather radar. Learning about the weather was probably what made this fear diminish and go away over time. The plus side of living in fear all those years was I became adept at reading the signs. I could tell if things were going to blow over or blow up in our faces.

We pushed through the door and I knew this storm wasn't blowing over.

The sky was a sickly green color, the rotation of the clouds overhead obvious as my old fears awakened. My feet stopped moving, their link to my brain severed by my near panic. My breathing sped up and even though I tried to regain some semblance of control, I could hear myself panting.

"Abbey."

I wanted to run. I couldn't move, though.

"Abbey!"

Someone was saying something. I felt far removed from the others in the group. My vision had closed up, all my peripheral was gone. I know I needed to move and get out of this storm. Even as the hail began to strike, I was frozen in place.

"Abbey. Are you with me?" My eyes took their time to focus on Turner's. His hands were on my face, his eyes inches away from mine. "Time for us to leave," he said with an unusual combination of calm and urgency.

He grabbed my hand, pulling me from my spot. Rather than get dragged by Turner, I gained strength from his touch and my feet regained their ability to move. We raced across the courtyard, feeling the sting of the marble-sized hail. I'd never experienced anything like that, the closest being the paintballs I was on the receiving end of at a church youth group outing last summer. I was definitely going to have welts again.

The door was just out of my reach as my hand stretched out. Time slowed as I looked at the door. Like most doors in older buildings, the door was a massive thing, made from oak, with rusted metal fittings. The surrounding wall was made of weathered river rock, cemented in place by craftsman a century before. A pattern in the oak beam caught my eye. The wood grain was long and fluid, almost like liquid as it curved and flowed like a river. In the darkest part of the grain, there was a symbol similar to the ones I'd seen around the school. There was something about the artful curve, the way it flowed, the fluidity...

The moment was gone as the door opened in front of me and I found Stacia and Carrie waiting inside for us.

"That hail is going to leave a mark," Turner said as he pulled off his T-shirt. The rest of us just sort of stopped what we were doing—thinking, moving, breathing, like that—while a now shirtless Turner wrung out his soaked shirt, twisting it in his hands. The corded muscles stood out in his arms while his six-pack tensed with his effort. Good lord, I don't think I'd ever seen someone so lean. The shirt was soon pulled back over his head and Turner looked around at our faces. "What?" he asked, clearly not getting it.

Carrie cleared her throat, pulling us back to the reality of our lives. "The clue..." She let her words hang there.

I tried my best to string together some coherent thoughts. However, "The gym. The rope. Climbing," was the best I could do. In my defense, 14-year-old girls were going through considerable changes. I'd be the first to admit the link between our brains and our bodies haven't been solid to begin with. But throw hormones into the mix and look out. These days, our bodies had become fiercely independent and were likely to betray us at the drop of a shirt.

The gym was mostly dark; the only light left burning was the center spotlight. But our goal was clearly lit: the scroll hung a foot or so from the ceiling. Four ropes hung in a circle surrounding it. There were two shorter lengths of cord lying on the ground below.

"I got this one," Turner said and began to climb the rope with ease. The higher he got, though, the easier it was to see he was too far from the scroll to reach it. Turner figured out the same thing and paused a few feet from the gym's ceiling.

"Try swinging," Carrie called up to him.

"Good idea," he replied, shifting his weight to start his swinging motion. Turner was at full reach but was still a good five feet away from the scroll. The issue was, when you were so close to the ceiling, you didn't have enough rope to move very much. He tried dropping another five feet and tried swinging again. This time, he had more movement, but then he was too far below to grab our clue.

"Try this," Carrie called and tossed up one of the lengths of cord we found on the floor.

Turner gave a valiant effort using the cord as a whip to knock the scroll loose. But he still wasn't able to get close enough to hit it down. And after a few more tries, he slid down.

"My arms are on fire," he said, shaking them. "I can't hold on and swing the rope well enough to knock the scroll loose. It looks to be secured pretty well." Turner's gaze lowered. I hadn't expected this— Turner looked embarrassed by his failure on the ropes.

"Better than we could have done," I said trying to give him some pride back. "But now what?"

"I have an idea," Carrie said, picking up a section of rope. "Stacia, hang onto the other end while we climb." She gestured for Stacia to climb the rope diagonal from hers.

Carrie held the end of her cord and used it to pull herself closer to Stacia. They were still too far, but I saw what they were trying to do and that gave me an idea.

"Hold on," I said. "C'mon on down. I have an idea."

There had to be a reason for the second length of cord and the two other hanging ropes. "Let's loop this around the other the cord like this." It was sort of like making a + sign. My cord started at the bottom at 6:00 and crossed theirs making a right angle turn ending at 3:00. Stacia got it and switched to the 9:00 position with Carrie in the 12:00 spot. Turner held the other end of our cord.

"Brilliant," he said. "This way we're pulling ourselves into the middle to release the scroll. They said we would have to work together. Teamwork, what a concept."

Turner stopped talking as he realized we were all staring at him. "I'm babbling, aren't I? My bad."

Making my way up the ropes, I clenched the cord in my teeth—it was just too difficult to hold it and climb at the same time. At the top, we pulled on our respective ends, tightening our group and bringing us closer to the scroll. Turner had the longest reach and was soon able to untie the scroll from its rope. He held it out for us to see and then dropped it to the floor below. "Last one down is a loser," he said as he started back down.

Carrie was the first to the floor after dropping the last six feet. Turner and Stacia were right behind. I was the last by a country mile, but I didn't care. My hands were raw, my biceps burned, and my shoulders were threatening to detach themselves from their sockets. I was just thankful to be on the ground again. Carrie held up her thumb and index finger to her forehead giving me the near-universal "loser" sign. Not one to be outdone, I held up a single finger, giving her the universal "I hope you have a long and happy life" sign. Or something like that.

Carrie slid the blue ribbon from the rolled up paper. The light from the spotlight illuminated the words.

> *If this place were smaller, a college it would be.*
> *Seeing it's not, my best advice would be*
> *To stay as far as possible from the edge.*
> *Searching for clues here can bring you up or bring you*
> *   down.*

"What's larger than a college? A university," Stacia said as she answered her own question, her smile wide and her eyes twinkling. Stacia may have her theatrical moments as she explored her Truly self, but she wanted to be accepted as much as the rest of us.

"You know, you're much smarter than your know-it-all sister. And better looking too." I told Stacia, giving her a wink.

"Where has Truly been?" Carrie asked. "I don't remember seeing her when they gave out our team assignments." Carrie didn't get it, but I did.

"I think we've seen the last of her pale blue sweater," I said giving Stacia a grin. "Truly has retired from public viewing. Elvis has left the camp." The astonished look on her face was priceless. In response to her questioning look, I just smiled and nodded. *Yes, I know your little secret.*

"Stay away from the edge as far as possible," Carrie paraphrased our clue. "What's far from the edge?"

"The middle?" I offered hesitantly.

"Ahh. So what's in the middle of the University?" Turner asked. "We need a map, because knowing our clue writer, we'll need to find the geographic center of the entire campus."

Stacia held up her hand. Always one for the drama, she left it there waiting for our full attention. "Turner mentioned the geographic center. The center is also far from the edge. And get this: the University Center." I honestly think she wanted to take a bow.

We all seemed to get it at the same moment: the clue was directing us back to the University Center. And we were off running for the door, anxious to get the next clue.

That was until I got to the door. I so didn't want to go back out there in the storm. Turner stepped up again to be my savior. "Do you trust me?"

I nodded.

"Then all you have to do is hold my hand."

I could do that. In fact, I liked doing that. A lot.

"Soon as we step outside, we're going to run like the wind. That's it. You don't worry, you don't stop, you just think about getting to the University Center and figuring out the rest of our clue. It was something about bringing us up or down. Focus on that, okay?" His eyes held mine, my fingers intertwined with his. Yes, I would follow this boy wherever he led. Who cared about a little bit of bad weather?

25

THE NUTCRACKER SUITE

I don't remember much about the weather. The hail had stopped, but the gusts of wind made me feel like I was a kite, fighting a losing battle to stay in one place. I simply held onto Turner's hand, allowing him to lead me through our weather apocalypse while I let my thoughts run free. The answer had come to me before we reached the end of the sidewalk. There was only one clear answer to the clue. What would be in the University Center that could bring you up or bring you down? See? It was obvious. The elevator.

It's good to be brilliant. However, I've found it tough to remain humble.

As we made our way through the storm to the University Center, I remembered seeing the distant silhouette of a group running in the opposite direction. I couldn't be certain because the lightning flash gave only the most fleeting glimpse, but there looked to be five of them. Why five? That number stuck with me as we made it to the welcome sanctuary of the University Center.

I pointed a finger toward the elevator, as a drop of rainwater fell from the tip. "The clue is in the elevator."

Turner stabbed a finger at the call button. The button lit up informing us the elevator had been summoned. Carrie arrived next and the first thing she did was push the already lit button. It might be human nature for each of us to have to push the elevator call button. I'm sure I'd done the same thing at some point in my life. Though, because it was Carrie, it bugged me.

"So, you didn't think Turner pushed the elevator button

correctly?" I asked, letting some of my irritation creep into my normally pleasant voice.

"Well, duh," she answered without hesitation. "If he had, the elevator would already be here, wouldn't it?" Carrie can give as good as she gets.

Leave it to Stacia to take things further. She stepped over to the elevator panel and gave it a series of quick jabs. "You clearly do not have the touch either." At that precise moment, the elevator chime sounded announcing its arrival.

We looked at each other and broke out laughing. Maybe it was the near-constant tension, maybe it was the weather or maybe it was our pent up frustration with each other, but we all broke out laughing. It was the kind of near hysterical laughter where you lose control of your body and find it's impossible to stay standing. ROFL is how I would text it.

The elevator opened while we were laughing and no one could make it inside before the door closed again. It was a good thing the door closed—although I don't believe the others saw what was on the elevator. A stern looking older man had pointed a finger directly at me. He was trying to convey something, but his meaning wasn't clear.

"Why did it leave?" Stacia asked. The elevator motor started and the indicator light above showed it had moved up to the second floor. "Is there someone up there who pushed the button? What if they took our clue?"

Carrie was at the elevator call button in a flash. I felt the tension eating at us as the elevator descended again. Turner pushed his way to the front, wanting to be there first when the doors opened. I hoped the elevator would be empty as I didn't want that angry man jabbing his finger at me again. While it hadn't exactly been unusual having dead people around me, there was something different going on there. Something with a greater sense of urgency.

The door opened. I held my breath. Turner had his arms up like he was ready to tackle whoever was after our clue. But the elevator was empty—not even a finger-waving, stern-looking older man. We crowded into the elevator car, looking up, looking down, and yet not finding the scroll.

"Damn," Turner spat out.

"Did you expect it to be sitting out in the open?" Stacia said. "Things haven't been exactly obvious so far. Maybe in here," she said, opening the elevator's emergency phone box. Stacia lifted the phone and looked behind it. The scroll wasn't in the phone box.

Turner had his eyes fixed on the ceiling of the elevator. He jumped and pushed at the ceiling tile with his fingertips. His first touch raised the tile before it settled back into position again. His second jump left the tile askew, white fiber sprinkling down on us like a December snowfall. His third jump dislodged the tile sending it to the floor in pieces. No scroll. Now what?

"Hello?"

All of us spun around to find Stacia with the elevator phone to her ear. She repeated the single word. "Hello?" Stacia's brow furled as she held up her hand requesting our silence.

"Time is your friend as you search for this clue." Stacia's voice had a monotone quality as she spoke. She paused, wanting us to remember our verbal clue. "Though getting fired at camp would bring you up to nine, not ten."

A long pause.

"That's it. They hung up." Stacia returned the phone to the box.

"How did the clue begin?" I asked.

"Time is your friend—our friend, I guess." Carrie paused, clearly having a thought on the clue. We paused and waited for her to continue. "I think it must be related to a clock," she said.

"Sounds like that might be it," I offered as we stepped off the elevator. "There's a clock outside the gym. The one that chimes at random times."

"It does?"

"I've never heard it do that."

"Me neither."

Whatever. Apparently, the clock chimed just for me on my first day here. Okay, I know what you're thinking, what's one more strange thing in a very strange life? But why? Why does it always have to happen to me?

"Hey," Turner said, bouncing in his spot. "It also said getting fired at camp would bring you up to nine, not ten. It must mean the nine o'clock position. The clue is at the nine." He smiled. "Let's go."

The group moved toward the entrance, eager to find the clue.

"Excuse me," I called, still standing outside the elevator. "I don't want to rain on our parade, but what's the deal with getting fired at camp? That doesn't fit with the clock thing."

The other three looked at me, slightly crestfallen. Actually, they looked at me like I was the older sister at the birthday party letting the air out of the kid's balloons. I know, I was such the fun sucker.

"Fired at camp?" Carrie spat. "How could we get fired at camp?"

"I know," I offered. "They won't let us leave. I even hired a lawyer, but no luck."

Ignoring me, Carrie was thinking out loud again. "Hmm, fired. At camp. Fired. Camp."

"OMG," Stacia said, with a huge emphasis on the G.

"What?" Turner was looking at Stacia, as most of us would look at the village idiot when he yelled about enormous floating blue elephants attacking city hall.

"Campfire. The campfire is laid out in a circular pattern, remember?"

She was right. I remember thinking the twelve huge tree stumps looked like the face of a clock. "Eureka! You nailed it. The leader stump is larger than the others too. That's our 12:00."

We raced for the door and I heard Carrie say "Eureka" under her breath. I wasn't altogether sure if she was mocking me or trying the word on for size. Either way, the word fit.

When we stepped into the night, the rain had stopped, the hail had disappeared and outside of the frequent lightning flashes, it was a beautiful evening. The lightning made the courtyard resemble the set of a movie. And I don't mean a feel-good romantic comedy type of movie. I mean a scare you so much you're peeking through your fingers, too scared to look, too scared not to look type of movie. You know the genre, where the crazed stalker with the hockey mask terrorizes a group of college students. Yeah, it felt a lot like that. But on the plus side, the rain had stopped.

Getting to the campfire site at Glenn Park meant crossing the swing bridge again and the idea of traversing that bridge tonight scared me. Those bridges weren't safe. When have you seen one of these in a movie and something hadn't gone horribly wrong? The rope snapped, the plank broke and suddenly someone plummets to their untimely death. I didn't want to be that person.

Yet, I was the first to cross. I gave directions for Stacia to follow when I was two-thirds across. It wasn't an accident I chose Stacia to follow—she was the lightest member of our group. No way was I sharing the swinging rope bridge of death with Turner, who must weigh at least 50 pounds more than me.

"I Can't Go For That," picked that moment to pop into my head. Another Eighties gem from Hall & Oates, the song caused me to freeze as I repeated, "no can do."

My main issue became apparent: it was difficult to keep moving when you had a death grip on the rope railing and your fingers had absolutely zero inclination to loosen up. It was clear my fingers had an unusually strong instinct for self-preservation. The only way I made it across was through the power of positive thinking and telling myself, *You can do this. You CAN do this.*

Oddly enough, the others appeared to have little-to-no difficulty navigating the narrow deathtrap. Maybe they weren't as tuned into the other side. Go figure.

Without the light from our usual comforting fire, long shadows obscured the campfire site at Glenn Park as the night reclaimed the grounds. Not wanting to prolong our time here at camp spooky, we headed directly for the stumps. Orienting myself, I pointed out, "There's the leader stump. That's 12."

We move counterclockwise. "11."

"The clue said 9, not 10."

"Here. 9:00. This is where it should be." We gathered around the stump, running hands along the rough sides feeling for our clue in the darkness.

I sensed it before I heard it. We were not alone out there.

If there was one thing you probably have learned about me by now, odd things are attracted to me. The once-in-a-lifetime happening, well, that's a Monday for me. The bizarre appearance of some unknown entity, welcome to my Tuesday. Wednesday will bring something equally strange—and you don't even want to know about the rest of my week. I had no idea why I was such a magnet to this type of thing, but to dispute the obvious would get me nowhere.

I knew we faced an imminent threat, as clearly as most would know there is a seed stuck in their teeth. What was unclear was the nature of the threat. I needed to know who or what we were up against. Standing up, I scanned the surrounding darkness.

Figures glided in the shadows, circling us, always moving, like a wolf pack stalking prey. I couldn't make out who—or what—they were. Strangely, a number popped into my head. Five.

There were five of them out there. I remembered catching a glimpse of five figures earlier outside of the University Center. The fact we were put into groups of four must have jarred something in my head, my brain taking note of the oddity. Why would there be five when we were put into groups of four? What I didn't know was if the five are from our world—or from the next. What I did know was there were only four of us.

"Guys," I said quietly. "We are not alone out here." I didn't think the others had picked up on the danger yet.

There was a shuffle of gravel off to my left. "Death awaits you all with sharp, pointy teeth." The voice quiet, barely above a whisper.

Behind me, Stacia made a noise like a whimper. I didn't turn around.

"What is it?" Turner asked.

"I'm not sure," I said as the figures steadily circled us.

"What do you want?" Carrie called out.

"Death." The whisper was off to my right this time.

"Sharp." My left now.

"Pointy." The whisper was behind me.

"Teeth." Directly in front of me now.

I considered myself a student of pop culture. I read *People*, surfed the entertainment blogs, watched a lot of cable TV and caught some classic movies. A favorite of mine was the hilarious *Monty Python and the Holy Grail*. Towards the end of the film, there was this great scene where the brave knights faced a killer bunny. The knights quickly realized they were over-matched and amid shouts of "run away," they did exactly that. I remembered the lesson well, knowing there would be times when, faced with insurmountable odds, the best course of action may well be a strategic retreat. I have to say, at that moment, my fight or flight instinct strongly tipped in one direction.

A random thought popped into my head. In the same film, a strange little man had warned Sir Robin and his brave knights of the killer bunny. "Death with nasty, large pointed teeth."

Now hold on for a moment. It wasn't ghosts we heard, but I did smell something fishy here. "Tommy?" I called out.

"There is no Tommy, only death," the voice hissed.

"You are such an idiot," Stacia said with a laugh. "Tommy, I would know your arrogant voice anywhere. Nice try."

A solitary figure separated from the shadows. It was Tommy—the jerk. Stacia and I got a solemn nod, while he gave Carrie an appraising look. He totally ignored Turner. There was no love lost between those two.

It was then that I noticed the scroll in Turner's hand. "You found the clue?"

"Yep," Turner said. "Let's move."

Stacia stood in front of Tommy, hand on hip, bouncing side to side, giving what I assume was her best flirting move. "Sorry, hun, we gotta go. We have a contest to win." She pushed past him.

"Hey, Tommy," I said as I followed Stacia. The other four boys stepped out from the shadows. Standing behind Tommy, they looked less than friendly.

Carrie and Turner were behind me. They eyed Carrie up and down while she returned their gaze with an aloof appraisal. With a dismissive eye roll, it was obvious they didn't meet her standards. As Turner attempted to follow her, the boys closed ranks around him. "He stays," Tommy said, putting a hand on Turner's chest.

He wasn't the same charming soccer boy we met in the cafeteria. Gone were his ready smile and flirtatious manner. What remained was a lot darker than I had seen before. As Tommy glared at Turner, the muscles in his jaw clenched, his tension mounting. There was a rising storm of malice in him threatening to erupt at any moment. For his part, Turner held his ground, neither provoking nor turning away from the threat facing him.

I realized there was more going on here, more than just super-charged testosterone coming to a head between those two. I sensed an outside influence; something was unquestionably interfering here. But where was it coming from?

Over the years, I've come to believe another dimension coexisted alongside ours. But this dimension was inhabited with the deceased who have not yet found their way or who have returned for some purpose only they know about. This dimension wasn't just a transitory place for dead people—there were other things... I've caught the occasional glimpse of dark fleeting shapes and terrifying figures watching from the shadows: the stuff of nightmares.

Don't get me wrong, there was more to this dimension. Wherever there's shadow, there has to be light. I've glimpsed beings there that filled me with indescribable warmth, leaving a serene peace nothing short of a tornado plucking me from the ground and sucking me into the darkness could possibly break.

Most of the time, this dimension parallels ours, not intruding into ours, but not all the time. Some of the inhabitants are stronger than others, and these are constantly seeking weaknesses, searching for a way into our world. When a vulnerability is discovered, they exploit it, often finding a vibration tuning them into our world. And this allows them to influence and interfere with the living.

I once met this otherwise normal girl who used a razor blade to cut her arm, opening her skin repeatedly after the wound began to heal. When I asked her why, she wasn't able to give me an explanation. This self-mutilation made no sense until I saw something looking back at me from her eyes. There was a dark fury staring at me, challenging me. What I saw in her eyes was not from our world—at least not from the world most people live in.

Sadly, this was exactly what I saw in Tommy. Something was exerting control over him. But, what was this new Tommy capable of? How ugly could this get? A violent reaction from him was certainly on the table. Protecting Turner had to be my priority—he had no idea what was actually happening.

"Tommy, hun," I said, stepping up to his side. I ran my hand down along his arm, feeling the cords of his muscle tense. I was ignored as he continued his stare down with Turner. I needed to break his concentration, disrupt his focus before things got ugly. Giving Tommy's bicep a hard squeeze, I continued. "You have such large muscles—for a soccer player."

My obvious sarcasm had the desired effect as Tommy's head turned in my direction. I pushed on Tommy's right arm with my left and just as he turned towards me, I brought my knee up as hard as I could. I'd seen this done in the movies and was hoping it would have the same effect. It did.

Based on the sound he made as he collapsed to the ground with both hands shoved between his legs, Tommy was in some discomfort.

I pointed a finger at the closest of Tommy's buddies and growled, "You don't want to mess with me. Not this week."

The boy looked shaken and held up his hands. The others took a step back, no longer looking me in the eye. There was no fight left in these guys. That was okay, 'cause I was done with them anyway.

26

DON'T YOU JUST LOVE DARK BASEMENTS IN DESERTED BUILDINGS?

We were still laughing a block later. "You were amazing," Stacia said.

Even Carrie seemed impressed. "I had no idea you were so tough," she said. "He won't be getting up anytime soon."

"Unbelievable," Turner said. "What was up with that guy? I've never liked him, but he was acting so bizarre."

"Could be the bad weather bringing out the worst in him," I offered. "I had an uncle who used to cry every time it snowed."

"Really?"

"Yeah. He was depressed half of the year. The other half of the year he was so worried about the upcoming winter, I don't think he was ever really happy. He finally listened to the rest of the family and moved to Florida."

"Did that help?"

"I don't know. He was run over by a bus his first day there."

Stacia looked at me, a scowl on her face. "And this entire time I believed you were the odd one in your family."

"At least we got the clue. I might have to kick their butts again if I have to go back there."

"Hold on killer, I have it," Turner said, holding up the scroll with a smile. This ribbon wasn't blue like all the others, it was red. He slid the ribbon off. "I guess this is our final clue of the hunt," he said.

We crowded around to read the verse as Turner unrolled the scroll.

You shouldn't throw stones if you're mad,

And happy people won't climb this tree,
Don't worry about the final answer you seek,
You will find it low in the NW corner.

Huh?

"That is so obvious," Carrie said.

I was missing something then. "It is?" I asked her.

"Well, duh. If happy people won't climb a tree, who will? Crabby people, that's who. Crab tree. Crabtree Hall. There you go," she said rather smugly.

"Isn't the building off limits? I'm pretty sure it's posted as closed for construction." Stacia said.

"You know, I thought I remember seeing a sign to that effect," I offered, thinking of our earlier visit there. "Would they send us into a building that's closed for construction?"

"It does seem unlikely," Turner said.

I decided to approach the clue logically. "What about the throwing stones part? What does that have to do with Crabtree Hall?"

"I'm sure it's just a throwaway line to get us from the mad people to the happy people part. You're reading way too much into this," Carrie said, arms folded, as she stepped into my space, staring me down. Carrie could be one intimidating bitch when she wanted to be. Fine. Whatever.

"Crabtree Hall it is then," I shrugged.

What kind of person throws stones? The question ran through my head as we broke into a run for Crabtree Hall. Not exactly looking like it came out of a travel brochure, the building looked decidedly ominous in the lightning flashes. The windows were all black, with just a faint glow coming from the front entrance.

My breath caught in my throat as I recognized a familiar slime-green glow coming from an upper-level window. The symbol was back.

The glow was faint at first, but rapidly became bright, as if someone had turned the dial way up. I glanced at the others to gauge their reaction, but they didn't appear to notice. Turning back, the symbol was now in every single window of the entire building and burning so brilliantly, I found myself squinting as I took in the mystery before me. The others—completely oblivious—moved up the sidewalk to the entrance. I admit it, I was more than a little freaked out.

The brilliant glow rapidly dimmed and faded from sight altogether as we approached the entrance. Okay, message received. If only I knew what it meant. A random thought popped into my tired brain. People who live in glass houses shouldn't be throwing stones.

Carrie slipped off her backpack and dropped it by the front steps. "We shouldn't need this," she said, pushing past the buildings closed for construction sign and lifting the yellow caution tape at the entrance. If I didn't know better, I would think they were trying to tell us something. But closed or not, we were going inside.

The faint light I saw earlier in the entrance was a construction light hanging over a wooden table littered with blueprints and coffee cups. We paused just inside the lobby area.

"Which way do we go?" Stacia said.

"The northwest corner."

"Which way is that?" Shrugs all around.

Turner stepped up to the table and peered at the blueprints. He twisted the plan around, sliding his finger around the paper getting his bearings. "Okay," he said looking up, "that way is north, and west is that way," pointing down a dark hallway. Not exactly inviting.

Turner flipped up the blueprint, revealing another set underneath. "Hang on, there is a lower level. The clue said low in the northwest corner. It looks like the basement is where we are supposed to go."

Great. I love dark basements in deserted buildings. Good things always happen there. I've faced down a lot of terrifying things in the course of my short life. That didn't mean I have to look forward to seeing more. However, I remember a quote I once read in English class. *You become brave by doing brave things.* I turned on my way-too-small flashlight, leading the way into the darkness. Time to be brave.

The hallway was an obstacle course of ladders, tools, various pieces of construction equipment, and even segments of walls. Most of the floor and some of the walls had been stripped down to bare studs. This part of the building was getting much more than a facelift. I led the group down the hallway carefully, watching every step. The symbol showing up so prominently in the windows had felt like a warning. The trouble with the symbol was—besides giving me the willies—it didn't actually tell me anything. But, like any good girl scout, I'll do my best to be prepared for whatever cow dropped my way. That was all I could do.

The stairwell was as gloomy as a graveyard and my flashlight barely made a difference. The beam illuminated a tight circle at my feet, but when I aimed it down the stairs ahead of me, it was as if the darkness swallowed the light. The only way to navigate the stairs was to shine the light onto the step below and follow the light.

With each step down, the air felt colder around me. My internal spookometer edged up another notch or two. The others were behind me, quiet outside of their breathing. No one had said a word since we moved into the darkness leaving me to wonder if they had the same ill-at-ease feeling I did.

A metal door loomed in front of me. The door led into the basement level, and hopefully, our final clue would be there waiting for us.

Do you ever have a song just pop into your head? This time, it was the classic Eighties rock song, "You May Be Right," by Billy Joel. My mother would often play his *Glass Houses* album when she was cleaning up the kitchen. She said it gave her the energy to do her chores. Even though it has been several years now, I remember the CD cover. It had Billy Joel looking all tough in his black leather jacket, getting ready to heave a rock through someone's window. Mom said Billy Joel was trying to be edgier, but I think he was attempting to distance himself from his soft rock ballads. Either way, the recording had some decent tunes on it. Hmmm. Glass houses.

Hand on the doorknob; it hit me: we were in the wrong building. All the clues pointed in that direction. You don't throw rocks if you live in a glass house, and the university is well known for its research on crabapples. I'd forgotten about it, but there was a glass house on campus—a greenhouse used for crabapple research. I would bet my iPhone the greenhouse was where we should go, not this smelly old dungeon of a basement. But there was no reason not to check it out first, was there?

I pulled the door open with a supreme effort, as it creaked loudly, protesting every inch of the way. I'd guess the door hadn't been used for decades. The funny thing was, before coming to the camp and enduring the seemingly endless physical training sessions, I wouldn't have had the strength to muscle the door open. I wasn't saying I could punch out the Hulk, but I had muscles where I didn't before. I straightened my arm, checking out my bulging triceps in the light of my flashlight. Very nice.

"Um, Abbey?"

"Sorry." I pushed through the doorway and stopped. Though I felt someone bumping my backside, there was no way I was going further. Three figures waited ahead in the darkness. The first was an older woman. Her face lined and stern, hair severely pulled up into an old-fashioned bun, this woman could make a living as a librarian. The woman's clothes looked even more out of style than her hair, but it was difficult to be certain when you could see right through them. Her torso was mostly transparent—less in our world than in the next —but her head looked to be more solid. It was an eerie sight. The two figures flanking her were large men with folded arms. These men belonged to the shadows; it wasn't so much a matter of transparency, they simply didn't belong here in a world where there was light.

The woman raised her hand and stabbed the air with her finger. The gesture was clear: go back.

"Abbey?" The voice was Stacia's.

I looked around, my flashlight illuminating Stacia's, Turner's and Carrie's faces. There was little doubt they saw something too. The emotions slid over their faces like the "How am I feeling?" poster in Ms. Neuman's office. Shock, fear and wonder passed through in equal amounts. I reached out my hand, touching Stacia's arm. "What do you see?"

Stacia looked at me with an odd expression as she hesitated, and gestured past me, "There's a woman's head. I can't make out anything else; her body just fades away—except for her hand."

Turner spoke next. "I think there are others with her. I'm certain really—but I can't actually see them."

"She wants us to leave," Carrie said. "Maybe we should." Her voice trembled as she said this.

Stacia held my gaze. "Is this what you see, Abbey? There is an old woman here, right? I mean, you see this type of thing fairly often..."

I could feel Carrie and Turner's eyes on me. Not wanting to meet theirs, I kept my gaze on Stacia. "Yes, there's a woman here. And two others are standing behind her. I can't make out much beyond their shapes, but I believe they're men. I get the feeling they're here to bring power to the woman. But they don't want to be seen—they don't belong in our world."

Stacia's eyes were watery as she held mine for a long moment. "Have you seen the woman—or the men for that matter—before?"

I shook my head.

"What do you want to do?" she asked.

"I think we should leave. Now," I said firmly.

"But what about our clue?" It was Turner this time.

"It's not here. It's at the school's greenhouse."

Carrie's mouth hung open, but it was Stacia who asked the question. "Why didn't you say something if you knew?"

I held up my hands. "The thought just occurred to me as we got down here. I..."

That was the moment all hell broke loose—into our world.

Living in Minnesota, I've never experienced an earthquake.

Tornadoes, yes. Complete whiteout snowstorms, even with thunder, yes. I've been affected by floods, chased by a cloud of mosquitoes, been threatened by an angry bear and even been given the evil eye by a protective mother moose as I maneuvered my canoe past her and her calf in the boundary waters of northern Minnesota—but I've never been through an earthquake. Sure, I've seen them in the movies —with the violent camera shake, the protracted shudder of the ground heaving and the side-to-side pitching of the people involved.

This wasn't like that. At all.

The *boom* was all around us. I could feel it through the floor, up my legs, all the way to my teeth. This was almost immediately followed by a sudden and violent shake of the building, almost as if we were hit by something. But what?

Though no one was beside me, I heard a whisper right next to my ear. It was oddly intimate to have someone so close. I half expected to feel the warm breath in my ear, it was that close. It wasn't a "Careless Whisper" like George Michael sang about, though. It was more of a life-saving message, a warning of an imminent threat. There was only one word used. But it was enough.

"Run."

"Go," I yelled, propelling Stacia back through the doorway. "We have to go!" I grabbed Turner's shirt and put a hand on Carrie's shoulder, pushing them ahead of me. "Move!"

The explosion was massive. It was loud and it was catastrophic. I felt the shock wave as the concussion blew past the doorway. The deadly debris propelled by the concussion narrowly missed us as I went sprawling to the floor. In the process, the flashlight fell out of my hand and hit the wall, causing the light to wink out. Luckily, I no longer needed it to navigate. We now had a new light source: the explosion started a sizeable fire just around the corner from us.

It was close and burning tremendously hot. The heat of the flame quickly seared the paint on the doorframe.

"We have to get out of here. This building isn't going to be standing much longer." My voice ragged and loud as I shouted to be heard over the roaring fire. The stairwell filled with smoke, a thick, black cloud looking twice as toxic as an over-microwaved Hot Pocket. With only one way out, we hurried up the stairs. It wouldn't be long before the smoke reached us.

Instinctively, we grabbed hold of each other's hands, a human chain to get us through the darkness. Turner was in the lead, pulling me by the hand, Stacia was behind me holding my other hand in a near-death grip while Carrie brought up the rear. My mind flashed back to younger days, holding hands with the girls, singing, "Ring around the rosie. A pocketful of posies. Ashes, ashes. We all fall down." Katie, Jean and I rolling on the ground, giggling uncontrollably. Hannah Scout always first to her feet, shouting to do it again, do it again. Friends I haven't thought of for years, friends I haven't seen in forever. Friends I hoped to see again—in this life.

I trusted Turner as he led us up the stairwell. With nowhere else to go, we moved up the stairs to get to safety. Looking back over my shoulder, great billows of black smoke pumped into the stairwell. With each passing second, my vision got more and more obscured. It was becoming harder to breathe with all of the smoke. I choked as I tried to get air into my oxygen-starved lungs. Turner bent down, getting a breath of fresher air and I followed his lead, squeezing Stacia's hand so she got the idea too. For the next few moments, we were a weaving, dipping chain, as we attempted to survive the horrible situation.

My foot was confused as it reached up for the next step and found none. However disconcerting this may be for my foot, it was good news for me. We were finally at the landing, and it was just a quick run down the hallway to freedom. The stairwell had filled up with so much smoke I doubt we'd have made it up to another floor. Turner yanked open the door and we were almost out of there.

Or not. That is the trouble with life—it's never as simple as we might imagine it.

There was a wall of flame ahead of us.

27
HIGH STRANGENESS

I knew I should have bought that life insurance.

It was beginning to look as if my stay at camp was going to be shorter than I originally had thought. No matter how badly I wanted to leave, getting carted out in an ambulance or a hearse was not the way I want to go. When I go, I want to go my way.

At the moment, our options looked severely limited. There was absolutely no way we could go back into the stairwell and we couldn't go through the wall of flames either. The explosion's resulting fire had grown immensely, the flames had come up through the floor from the basement. How much longer could this building stand?

Carrie pushed open a door into one of the dorm rooms. "The window," she yelled. "We can get out through the window." There was a roar coming from the hallway as the fire consumed everything in its path—a path we appeared to be in. Me? I'd like to choose the path less traveled. The window it was.

Unfortunately, the window didn't open—it was just a large double-thick piece of glass. I guess they didn't want the college students sneaking out at night. Our situation became even direr, as smoke flooded the room—the fire right outside the door. Turner slammed his shoulder into the window trying to break the glass. Nothing happened. He took several steps back and ran at the window. The glass bowed a bit, but the only real result was Turner being flung to the ground. He looked dazed as he got back to his feet. The flames licked at the doorframe, not quite into our room, as they curled around the edge. Clearly, we didn't have much time left.

"The Heat is On," Glenn Frey's Eighties song popped into my

head and I knew I had to do something soon. Close to panicking, I frantically looked around the room for something to break the glass. This was a construction site, there had to be something we could use to bust the window open. But the question was, would busting out the window send a load of oxygen into a hungry fire? The answer was clear; we had no time and we had no choice.

I spotted a bucket at the base of the scaffolding set up along the far wall, handles sticking up out of the bucket. I raced over, hoping to find a hammer. Against all odds, I glanced up to see an opening right through the ceiling.

"Hey," I called. "Forget the window. We can climb right out of here."

Stacia ran over and just like that, she moved like an Olympic athlete up the scaffolding. It was amazing what you can do when you're properly motivated. Carrie and Turner started up after her. Stacia has no trouble whatsoever making it through the opening. Turner had to work at wriggling through, and I had the impression Stacia was pulling from overhead.

In a moment he made it through, followed by Carrie. I was struck by the similarity to our obstacle course as I made my way up. A last glance down showed me the fire had entered the room. Time to make my escape.

Hands waited for me as I reached through the opening and I'm pulled up to the second floor. In a decidedly awkward moment, we all embraced in a group hug. It felt so good as tears ran down my cheeks. After an uncomfortably long moment, we let go and backed away from each other.

The room was pretty much the same as the one below with a noticeable difference: there was no fire. We may have bought ourselves some time, but not a lot.

We made our way into the hallway, relieved not to find the fire there—yet. I still smelled smoke, but it was probably just me. You know how you smell all smoky when you get home from a bonfire? It was like that—only a thousand times worse. The others looked both wet and sooty, and I was sure I looked just as lovely. But hey, this was a scavenger hunt, not a beauty contest. However, at least for us, the hunt was over. Now it was a very real game of survivor. And this was not a game I wanted to lose.

"We need to get back down to the main floor," Turner said. "It's our only way out. Let's go to the far stairwell and make our way down. It should be far enough from the fire. Are you with me?" he asked, looking at each of us.

I nodded my head along with Carrie and Stacia. What other option did we have?

Running down the hallway, I knew there wasn't any way my father was sending me back to camp next summer. Not if I had a say in the matter. And now that I have my own lawyer, Brian Thompson, Attorney-at-Law, I had double the say. Look out, Dad.

We just passed the elevator bank when I saw it again. I hit the brakes and yelled, "Hold it!" at the top of my lungs. When Turner heard me, he reluctantly stopped and reversed direction.

"What is it?" he asked, looking a little wary of the ghost girl. Even though it was my role in our crisis, being that girl had cost me more friends than I could count on both of my hands. I didn't want to lose these friends, but I didn't want to die either. So, I couldn't ignore a warning when I found one. Turner stepped closer, a questioning look on his face. I simply nodded at the door adjacent to the elevator.

The mysterious symbol—a sickly shade of green—glowed brightly on the door. The curved backward letter f, with the dot at the bottom right, looking as if it was hacked into the door with an ax—not delicate and definitely not subtle. "Look at the way it's glowing," I said. "It has to mean something, doesn't it?"

Carrie reached out a tentative hand toward the mysterious mark. As her finger made contact with the door, something decidedly odd happened. The glow jumped from the symbol and attached itself to her fingertip. Carrie uttered a frightened moan but left her hand where it was.

Time ground to a halt. My breath was caught in my lungs as I took in the high strangeness unfolding in front of me.

The glow expanded engulfing Carrie's entire finger, then gaining speed as it took over her hand up to the wrist. She turned with terrified eyes, pleading with me to make it stop. But there was nothing I could do as it rapidly moved up her arm. Her T-shirt sleeve fluttered and bulged out as the glow had seemingly taken on mass. It moved higher up her outstretched arm, almost to her shoulder. Carrie's sudden, piercing scream galvanized us and sent time back to its normal pace.

As one, we all moved to help her. Stacia had her hand around Carrie's waist pulling her back, while I slapped her hand away from the door and the strangely consuming symbol. At the same moment, Turner made a full body tackle to get her away from the door. The result was we were all thrown to the floor, a tangle of bodies, as we rolled into the opposite wall with a bone-jarring thud.

Before we could get to our feet, another massive shudder rocked the building. Without warning, the end of the hallway collapsed. No explosion, the ceiling simply buckled and fell into the hallway, causing the floor to give way. Flames engulfed much of the falling debris, as though another fire had been raging on the top floor as well. The noise reminded me of a locomotive bearing down the track at full speed. When the roar was over, the entire end of the building was a jagged tear, exposing the building to the night.

I couldn't even begin to describe the sight of the lightning flashes as they lit up the hallway. The rain pelted the hall's interior, sizzling as the drops struck the smoldering debris of what was just recently the third floor.

"Oh my God," Carrie said, "Abbey, if you hadn't stopped us..." Her words trailed off.

Turner was getting to his feet. "We'd all be dead," he said finishing Carrie's thought.

Maybe it wasn't so bad being the ghost girl, after all.

28

LOUD WOMPF SOUNDS ARE NEVER A GOOD THING

What do you do when everything is crumbling down around you?

No, I wasn't speaking figuratively or even metaphorically. I meant the entire frickin' building was on fire and falling down around me. Literally.

"We've got to get out of here." Carrie said this matter of factly—as if we hadn't all been thinking the same thing. "This firetrap won't be standing much longer."

"Yeah, but how?" Turner asked, a look of near panic colored his face. "Every way we go is another dead end."

I held his eyes for a long moment, willing him to feel my calm. I glanced at the others. "You're going to have to trust me. I believe I can get us out."

"But how?" Carrie asked.

"I think we've been getting some help and I've got to trust we won't be led down the wrong path." My fingers were crossed for good luck, but I wasn't going to share my superstition with the others. "We start with this door," I said, hand on the knob. The symbol glowed as brightly as when we first saw it.

"Are you nuts?" Turner asked. "No offense, but why are you trusting whoever is sending these messages? Why would someone—or something—want to help us? You're too trusting for our own good."

"Suppose they want you to cross over to be with them? That seems more likely," Carrie said and paused, a decidedly awkward pause. "Just saying."

My tears welled up, wanting to flow, but now wasn't the time. "Let me ask you this," I said, looking at Carrie. "What choice do we have?"

Blank looks of indecision all around. That's what I thought. "Come with me if you want to live." I always wanted to say that. I pushed open the door and stepped into the darkness.

WE SEEMED to be out of options. We were on the second floor, with one floor above, a massive fire spreading alarmingly fast on the two levels below. The building was laid out with stairwells on opposite ends and one in the middle, located next to the elevator. We were at the middle stairwell and the only path to escape was on the first floor, so we automatically turned to the descending stairs. But, large metal drums filled the landing below, making it difficult to pass through.

I glanced up, and spotted the now familiar symbol emblazoned on the wall above the flight of stairs. "We need to go up," I said, grabbing Stacia's hand and pulled her toward the greenish glow of the symbol.

Wouldn't it be easier if the ghostly messenger just put up some arrows instead? Same idea, right?

Life was strange. The symbol's glow had given a bizarre greenish-lime cast to the entire stairwell—making us look like some type of jello creatures. Strange times, indeed.

The mark began to fade as we approached the landing halfway up to the third floor. When my foot hit the landing, the symbol disappeared, leaving us in the dark. Confident we were being led up to the third floor, I shuffled to my left, outstretched hand sliding along the wall as I turned toward the rising stairs. Yes! The glow was burning brightly at the top of the stairs. It may have been the strangest beacon ever, but it was *my* beacon.

"C'mon, Stacia, we're almost there," I said as I grabbed her hand.

Without warning, there was a loud *wompf* sound below us. I don't know about your life experiences, but in mine, loud *wompf* sounds were never a good thing.

Those large metal drums blocking the landing... I wondered if those drums were filled with flammable liquids or chemicals. I'm no safety inspector, but storing 50-gallon drums of chemicals in a stairwell would be an obvious safety code violation in my book.

Turner headed back down the stairs. "Hang on," was all he said. We lost sight of him as he turned the corner. We looked at each other, not sure what to do. How long was he planning on being gone? We didn't exactly have much time.

It turned out he was thinking the same thing. Eyes blazing, Turner came around the corner, frantically gesturing at us.

"Run!" he shouted. The panic in his voice took away any indecision we might've been feeling. "Move, move" he shouted again. We didn't need to be told twice, we were running for our lives.

We busted through the symbol-marked door onto the third floor, anxiously scanning for another otherworldly mark. For me, this had become so much more than just escaping; I needed to know what the symbols meant. My mom used to talk about her harrowing experiences in South America. Being in such a strange land had frightened her at first, but as she often said, "Curiosity will conquer fear even more than bravery will." I got that now.

And because the symbol had shown up before our lives were in danger, it had to mean something beyond being our roadmap to safety. I wouldn't stop until I figured it out.

"There," I shouted. The symbol glowed on the wall not even ten yards away. As we raced toward the symbol, the mark faded as a new one lit up the wall another ten yards down on the opposite side.

There was smoke in the hallway, but with the building open to the night air, there was more than enough ventilation. Of course, the necessary components for fire—heat, fuel and oxygen—were now present in copious quantities. Ahead of us, the last third of the building was alive with dancing flames. Yet, this was the direction we were headed for.

The symbol faded as if someone was rapidly turning down the dimmer switch. Another ten yards down, the symbol grew in brilliance—from a door this time. With no hesitation, we hit the door, ramming it open. The room had been stripped down to bare studs, the flooring removed to the support beams. Stopping at the edge, I could see down into the second floor room below.

We knew what we had to do.

Stacia frantically unlooped great lengths of orange industrial-weight power cord, as Turner grabbed one end and raced over to the bare studs of the closest wall, looping it around the beam. Tying it off with three knots, Turner pulled it tight as he braced his shoe against the beam. Satisfied, he rejoined us as Stacia tossed the remaining length over the edge. "Go," he said, directing me to go first.

I grabbed the cord and fell through the opening. My hands, now used to climbing ropes, easily hung on as I rapidly slid down to the second floor, landing gracefully. Stacia followed, letting out a whooping cheer as she flew down. Leave it to Stacia to make the most of each moment. Carrie rocketed down and Turner practically jumped the whole way, using the cord to put on the brakes at the very last second, cushioning his landing.

Safely on the second floor, we continued our quest to find a way out of the building. Stepping out into the hallway, I sized up our options. The floor had been completely removed directly in front of us. Ten feet down the hall, the floor looked passable, but there wasn't any way to leap the gap. Turning to the others for ideas, I noticed the green symbol glowing on the wall behind Carrie. That was our exit.

"We have to go through the wall. The hall is blocked." The time for disagreement was long past and the others simply nodded and began to look for the appropriate tools to get us through the wall. The sledgehammer seemed just right and I grabbed the handle, surprised by the weight.

"Allow me," Turner said, and I relinquished my grip. To say

Turner attacked the wall would be an understatement. Zero hesitation, he launched himself at the wall, swinging the sledgehammer wildly. Fear and frustration fueled his intensity to Hulk-like savagery. The drywall didn't stand a chance. He was through with the first swing, the second swing created an opening large enough for us to squeeze through.

Turner's fury didn't readily release him from its ferocious grip. He pulled back for yet another hit and I stepped in, stopping him at the apex of his swing. "You've got it," I said gently. "Let's go."

He threw the massive tool to the ground, like *yeah, I'm done with you.*

The adjacent room was much the same. Stripped down, an opening to the room below—an opening to a room on the first floor. That could be our way out.

The door, however, had the symbol and I had to trust it. The smoke was thick out in the hall, almost as thick as it was in the stairwell. I took in a large gulp of air before stepping out into the hall.

Ahead, just over an arm's length away, another symbol was on the wall. With visibility so limited, I was thankful there was something about the quality of the glow that cut through the smoke, like how fog lights illuminate the way through the mist. Another symbol was on the opposite wall, and another opposite that. We weaved through the smoky corridor bouncing from wall to wall. After about the seventh wall symbol, I spotted it on another door.

This door was locked, but no way was that going to stop us. When you're as highly motivated as we were, a locked door was nothing. Turner stepped back, bracing himself against the opposite door. Everyone should know how to bust open a door by now, we've all seen the cop shows. Turner's technique was spot on, as he lunged forward and slammed his heel into the door next to the knob. The door flew open, the latch plate gliding across the room, bouncing off the wall. So cool.

Looking over the edge of the opening in the floor, I spotted the welcoming glow of the otherworldly mark down below—far below.

What wasn't so good was the fact the mark wasn't on the floor below, but on the floor below that.

We were being led back to the basement.

"Turner," I said, looking into his sooty face, the streaks looking much like a warrior's face paint before battle. The similarity wasn't lost on me, as we had been battling for our lives for the last hour. Honestly, it may have only been ten minutes—time felt irrelevant in circumstances like ours. "We have to go back down to the basement."

No argument. He simply nodded, holding up a flashlight. "I found this with the tools."

"That helps. Now we just need another cord. A really, really long cord."

Carrie came up with the power cord—yellow this time—and handed the end to Turner. Seconds later, I was freefalling into the abyss wondering where and how I was going to land. I recognized this as a metaphor for my life, just as another of my mom's sayings picked this moment to pop into my brain: "To expect the unexpected shows a thoroughly modern intellect." Believe me, with my life, I've always expected the unexpected.

It was an odd experience to rappel through a room and continue through the floor into the room below. I could only imagine the surprised looks I would get if someone was sitting in the first floor room, perhaps a man sitting in his overstuffed chair reading the paper, watching as I go shooting through his room. However, there wasn't anyone—alive at least—in the building. I gained speed as I headed for the basement level.

I hit the concrete floor of the basement with a bone-jarring jolt and stepped to the side as Stacia dropped through the ceiling hole. She was making her whooping sound again. Honestly, if we weren't in such danger, this might have been a little fun.

With Carrie and Turner's arrival, I searched for the symbol showing our way out. The smoke was thick, even though the fire wasn't right on top of us. With the building falling apart all around us and the fire consuming what was left, there wasn't a clear path out. We had to find the symbol to get out of there and soon.

As if to punctuate our pressing need, a loud creak turned into a groan which rapidly crescendoed into a full-blown roar. I spun around, totally stunned at what I saw. The ceiling had collapsed. It was massive; the entire end of the building where we first came down the stairwell resembled a landfill littered with the remains of construction materials. A compressor fell right in front of us, no doubt having been on one of the higher floors. It exploded on impact, launching a thousand pieces in our direction. One of the wheels hit just above my knee.

We were lucky we weren't killed then and there.

"Move," Turner yelled as he propelled me down the hall. "This whole building is coming down and we're underneath it all." A sprint for the finish, we raced away from certain death, with no idea where we were headed. The symbol hadn't yet shown itself down here.

We were roughly in the middle of the building, near the elevator and adjoining stairwell as we moved fast. There were more flames and a wall of debris ahead.

I almost missed it.

Down low, back in the dark, there was a familiar greenish glow. Even though the symbol itself wasn't visible, that scary, awful—yet wonderfully welcome—lime green glow was.

"Here," I called, as I hit my brakes. "It's down here."

Turner's flashlight lit the way. Past a sea of crates and decade's worth of stuff— because nobody knew what else to do with it other than shove it into the basement—sat a square metal door. Roughly three square feet in size, cobwebs completely framed the small door, showing us it had been likely decades since anyone had used the long forgotten door.

Yet, the symbol glowed through the cobwebs from that very door. The marks looked to have been made by someone who had a screwdriver and plenty of time as they dug scratches and grooves deep into the metal of the door. If I had done it, it would have taken well over an hour of painstaking time, scratching over and over, digging the pointy end of my screwdriver into the steel of the door. After that, I would've taken a can of green glow-in-the-dark paint and coated the etched symbol until it radiated brilliantly from the center of the image and a more diffused glow from the outer edges.

In case it wasn't obvious by now, clearly someone not from our earthly world had placed the symbol there.

29

A Ghost Girl Like Me

It was going to be gross and disgusting, but I knew exactly what I had to do.

"Let me go first," I offered and got no argument from the others. Down on my knees, I used the handle of Turner's flashlight to clear away the cobwebs until I was inches away from the door. When I was finished, I handed back the flashlight.

Turner made a face but didn't say anything when he touched the mat of sticky webs on his flashlight.

Reaching out with my right hand, my fingers inched tentatively toward the etched glow of the symbol. As it did with Carrie earlier, the glow jumped from the symbol and onto my fingers. With my frightened nerves screaming at me to pull away, I forced my fingers against the symbol as the sickly lime green color spread up my fingers, overtaking my entire hand and rapidly enveloping my arm. As the glow spread, I got a cold tingling sensation almost as if the warmth was getting sucked out of my skin.

"Abbey," Stacia gasped behind me.

But, I couldn't stop, realizing this was the only way. Inching forward, I pressed my palm flat against the symbol. The cold spread faster, moving up to my neck. I couldn't help but shiver as the glow completely covered the upper half of my body.

Even though my arm felt like it was in the early stages of frostbite, there was raw power in my touch. I squeezed my fist, enjoying the sensation. Grabbing onto the door's rusty handle, I trusted my otherworldly helper, twisting and pulling in one confident motion.

The second my hand touched the door, I knew—without a

shadow of a doubt—that I could open it. With a feeble, creaking protest, the door opened.

There was more going on here than I first suspected, as strange thoughts began to flood my head—faces, someone running, emotions, and different languages. Everything was going so fast, too fast to comprehend, as the film raced in my head. A whirlwind that only seemed to speed up. Images of foreign-looking faces, exotic locales, screams, pain. Hot. Cold. Darkness.

Willing it to stop, I focused my breathing, using the meditation techniques my mother taught me. The rush of intruding thoughts and memories slowed and went dim. It took everything I had, but I was able to push it all away. Shivering, I stretched my arm out into the tunnel, as the supernatural glow illuminated a surprising distance ahead. There was no end in sight, just shadows becoming darkness. There was no choice, though, this tunnel is where we had to go.

I was trying to avoid skinning my knees, but it was clearly a losing battle. Wearing shorts had seemed like a good idea at the time. There just wasn't room to move—other than the slow forward crawl I was already doing. Stacia, followed by Carrie and Turner, were behind me. Someone was crying, but as I couldn't turn around, I had no idea who it was.

"I still believe we can win this thing," I called out in an attempt to lighten the mood. "Really, the scavenger hunt is ours. I'm guessing none of the other teams have had the help we've had. And so what if we lose? Could extra physical training faze us after what we've been through? No frickin' way!"

Turner called up from the rear, "Mr. Johnson better not even try. I have some pranks I've been saving that will blow him out of the water. He won't know what hit him."

That-a-boy. Keep their minds off our situation. We had to stay focused on what was ahead. Never mind the collapsing firetrap we'd left behind or the dark, damp, and utterly claustrophobic tunnel we were trapped in. If we panicked in here, it could potentially be as dangerous as if we had stayed in the building. We just have to focus on getting out.

"A root beer would be good. What better way to celebrate than with a tall frosty mug?" Stacia said. "A root beer and maybe some french fries. Sounds perfect, doesn't it?"

Carrie chimed in, her voice lacking its usual confidence. "You know, I am thirsty. Breathing in so much smoke leaves a girl quite parched."

"I could go for an ice cream cone," I added. "Our favorite place is Nelson's Ice Cream in Stillwater. There's nothing else like it. The size of their cones is astonishing. A child's size cone would feed a family of four. And Stacia, they have root beer, too."

"Count me in."

"Me, too. So let's get out of here."

"Sounds good," Turner called. "Can you go any faster?"

"I'm trying," I replied. My bloody knees were moving as fast as they could.

And in his best Yoda voice, Turner answered, "Do or do not, there is no try."

I was tired, my knees were raw, my arms were sore, but the supernatural glow radiating from my hand hadn't diminished in the least. It continued to light the way. The tunnel felt as if it stretched on forever. I had absolutely no idea where we were, how far we'd moved away from Crabtree Hall—or even if we'd moved off campus. We could be across the Kinnickinnic River by now. Who can tell when you're deep underground?

I hoped I would see something different soon, some sign our underground journey was coming to an end.

And then, there it was. The tunnel had come to an end.

The shadows ahead closed in as I made out another steel door, a twin to the one behind me. I gripped the handle tightly and twisted.

Again, it opened easily, this time out into a chamber. Crawling through the doorway, I was relieved to find myself in a tall space with metal rungs attached to the sheer concrete wall. Extending my arm to light the way, there were a dozen of those metal steps and another door at the top. This had to be it!

Stacia's head popped out of the doorway. "What's going on, ghost girl?" No malice, no teasing, just her friendly banter.

I grinned at her. "Looks like we made it."

"I know, right?" She held out her hand for some help, and then seeing my glowing hand, pulled back. Not that I blamed her. "I got it," she said and pushed her way out.

Carrie took Stacia's offered hand and slid out of the tunnel. Her knees looked as bad as mine. "Nice work, ghostie," Carrie said, her face breaking into a grin.

I suppose I may have just taken on a new nickname. Understandable, considering I glowed like nuclear-radiated lime Jell-O.

"Thanks, Carrie. We're a good team, aren't we?"

"The best." Her eyes looked wet like maybe she was tearing up. You know, I could actually grow to like that girl.

"Hey, don't forget about me," Turner said as he poked his head out.

Stacia tousled his hair playfully and smiled. "Never, big guy. You da man. We couldn't have made it without you. Now, come on out so we can go collect our trophy."

Turner squeezed his wide shoulders through the narrow doorway and, standing, stretched to his full height. "I thought we would never get out of there. I will never watch another prison break movie where the prisoners tunnel out," he said, shaking his head.

I had to laugh. "Have you seen many prison movies?"

He shrugged. "Well, no. Just making a point, really." His voice trailed off.

"You are a goof, but I love you," I replied before realizing what I'd said. The others were quiet, shifting glances between Turner and myself. Talk about your awkward silences.

Turner was the one who broke it finally. "I love you too, ghostie." Which worked, as everyone cracked up. I was laughing too, but underneath the glowing green light, I was pretty sure I was all red with embarrassment.

30
SWEET RELIEF

I couldn't bring myself to open the door to freedom.
Even though I was confident this is door could get us out, I hesitated. What I wasn't so confident about, was how my supernatural glow would go over when others saw me.

Let me spell it out for you: for a 14-year-old girl, life was all about fitting in, not calling attention to yourself. Yeah, I get what you're thinking. Not being like everyone else should be a good thing. My dad liked to say, "To wish you were someone else is to waste the person you are." However, it was one thing having your own sense of style, but it was another thing altogether to be glowing like Dr. Frankenstein's Jell-O dessert, made after a long hard night in the lab.

Stacia, who appeared to be able to read me like a book, accurately understood my hesitation. "Abbey, it's going to be okay. What we've survived tonight is amazing. Don't let a little thing like a bit of extra color ruin things for you."

"Extra color? Extra color would be a sunburn, not this mutant glow. I look like one of those fish from National Geographic that lives in the dark at the bottom of the ocean."

"Let's just get out of here," Stacia said, sounding confident and reassuring. "We'll get it sorted out. Somehow."

Not quite so confident, I grabbed the handle and pushed the door open. Immediately, I was slapped in the face by an angry shrub. Willie the groundskeeper clearly hadn't been doing his job—the opening was overgrown with bushes. I had to fight to create enough of an opening for me to get through.

The night air smelled so clean and fresh—no small wonder

considering we were trapped in a burning building and forced to crawl through a moldy tunnel. As I climbed out, something remarkable happened. The glow simply faded and disappeared. Yes! I pumped an arm into the air, though deep down I was so relieved I could just cry. Some days it can be tough keeping it together. And this would be one of those days.

"Abbey, you're back to normal," Stacia said and gave me a welcome hug.

The Go-Go's had a song, "Our Lips are Sealed," which was exactly what I hoped for from my friends. I really didn't want word of what I could do to get out. I pictured being locked away in an underground lab and getting endlessly poked and tested by government scientists. I'd rather just go to school like everyone else.

"Hey guys, one thing before we go. Can we agree to keep my unusual abilities between ourselves?"

"Your secrets are safe with us, right?" Turner said as he looked at Carrie and Stacia. All nodded solemnly.

It was only then we noticed the sirens filling the night air. They were getting louder by the moment. It must be every fire truck in the entire county. One went screaming by, just over the rise of trees. More were coming.

"Let's go," Turner called over the wail of the sirens. Re-energized, we raced for the top of the hill. And stopped.

"Unbelievable."

"Whoa."

"We were in there?"

Standing side by side, at the summit, we were stunned at what was in front of us. We instinctively reached out for each other's hand. I wasn't even sure whose hands I held, but it didn't matter. Drawing on each other's strength, we tried to process what we saw.

Crabtree Hall was engulfed in flames, reaching a hundred feet into the air. Both ends of the building had completely collapsed. The middle section remained standing, but the top floor had collapsed onto the second floor. This was where the fire burned the hottest, whereas the ends looked to have mostly burned out. Smoke poured out of the rubble. Fire trucks surrounded the building, as the firefighters worked urgently to contain the fire. Police cars and medical vehicles were on the scene as well. A crowd of curious watched from the other side of the street.

Still stunned at the sight of the devastation before us, we tentatively approached the crowd from the back as we took in the commotion playing out across the street. The firefighter's efforts were focused on the middle section, and another two trucks arrived to join the fray. It was a spectacular sight to see the truck's ladder extended to the second story as a stream of water hit the fire.

I shifted position to get a better view of the action. People pointed as a firefighter ran up the sidewalk to the entrance. He scooped something up into his arms and raced away from the building as a portion of the second floor collapsed, raining debris onto the front steps. I joined the collective gasp of the crowd, stunned to see just how close to death the firefighter had been.

He joined the men directing the firefight at a red SUV parked askew on the curb. After a moment of collaboration, the firefighter was pointed across the street. He headed toward the crowd, still carrying something in his left hand. He paused long enough to remove his helmet and wipe the sweat from his forehead, concern evident on his face.

He was met by Mr. Kindle, Mr. Johnson and Ms. Neuman, as well as several of the camp staff. A crowd of ToughLove campers moved closer to hear what was said. Standing there in the back of the crowd, I couldn't hear anything. Whatever he was carrying was handed over to Mr. Johnson. Ms. Neuman moved closer, looking to see what it was. Her normally impassive face was colored with emotion and she wiped away tears.

A murmur rippled through the group. I wanted to know what was happening, so I whispered to the girl in front of me, "What's going on?"

Without turning around, she replies, "They found a backpack.

Guess one of the scavenger teams was inside when lightning struck."

Ahh. So that's what happened. Lightning would explain the enormous *boom*. For once my fear of storms had been validated. Oddly, I got no comfort from the thought. It took me way too long to overcome the paralyzing fear of bad weather. Fear was no longer welcome in my life. Besides, lightning never struck twice. The odds would be astronomical I'd endure another killer storm in my lifetime. You know what that means? From now on, I could live a charmed and stress-free life. Sweet.

Turner was beside me. I reached for his hand, and his strong fingers intertwined with mine. "What's happening?" he asked.

"They found a backpack. A scavenger hunt team was inside when the lightning struck. The fire was started by a lightning strike."

"That makes sense."

"Who was inside?" Stacia asked, joining us.

"Not sure. They found someone's backpack."

"Hey, that's my backpack," Carrie said, "I left it on the front steps."

OMG. "Guys, everyone believes we were in the burning building —they think we died in there."

Ms. Neuman's face held my attention. Surprisingly, she was crying. The entire time I'd known her, I wondered if she liked me at all. At times, she seemed so aloof and distant, while other times I thought she was mean. One thing I was confident about—seeing her sobbing in the midst of her peers—she was devastated at the news of our deaths.

I pushed my way through the group, knowing I had to go to her. Ignoring the stunned faces of the people I passed, I moved to the front of the group. Her head down, Ms. Neuman's body quaked with the emotion of her sobs. I reached out, touching her cheek, wiping away her tears. "I'm okay," was all I can think to say.

She lifted her head, shock and surprise giving way to sweet relief. She grabbed me and held on like she would never let go. It was a moment I won't ever forget.

31
I Am the Ghost Girl

"Un-frickin-believable!" I shook my head. "One week left."

For once, we hadn't been woken up at the crack of dawn, as our physical training regimen had been put on hold, possibly for the remainder of camp. Surprisingly, I was torn on this, because as much as I've disliked physical training, I wouldn't have survived last night without it. Cows will fall and you have to be prepared for it.

"One more week here at our favorite Camp ToughLove." Stacia was on her bed, looking straight up at the ceiling. "Our lives will never be the same."

I had to agree. The aftermath of our near-death experience had been overwhelming. When we were discovered, you'd think we threw the buzzer-beating, game-winning basket from half court. People were yelling, crying, lifting us up, and hugging us until I thought my insides were going to come out my ears. The crowd surrounded us as we told our story, each of us relaying portions of the journey through the burning building. Thankfully, no one made mention of the ghostly symbols road mapping our way out—which would have been nearly impossible to explain. The head firefighter looked a tad skeptical hearing we just happened to find the needle-in-a-haystack way out. "How would you even know it was there, let alone know it would take you out of the building?"

Lucky guess?

Mr. Kindle confirmed the clue was meant to point us to the greenhouse. And surprisingly, he agreed the clue was vague enough to point us to Crabtree Hall as well. The shocker came when he addressed the crowd, citing our teamwork as the model of how we should be working together for the common good.

"Harriet Beecher Stowe once said, when you get in a tight place and everything goes against you till it seems as though you could not hold on a minute longer, never give up then, for that is just the time and the place the tide will turn. These four embody that spirit better than any example I could dream of." Imagine, me, a positive role model.

The staff wanted us to go to the hospital, but we were having none of that. "I feel fine," each of had insisted in our own words. Really, none of us wanted to be separated. We'd been through too much together to go our separate ways. Even Carrie stood with her arm around me for support as the firefighters and camp administrators grilled us about the night's events. And to tell the truth, I was okay with her being so close. When you risk your life together, an unbreakable bond is created. Carrie will be my friend for life.

As we finally parted, we agreed we would meet up for breakfast the following morning.

"Hey, guys," Carrie and Turner popped their heads in our room.

"Carrie!" I yelled and crushed her with the passion of my hug. A week earlier, I would have bet a million dollars against our ever hugging, let alone voluntarily being in the same room. It's the near-death bonding thing again.

"Abbey!" she yelled, matching my forceful hug with the same maximum pounds-per-square-inch death grip. I had tears again, but it was okay, these were my friends.

"I'm here too," Turner said, looming next to us. Carrie and I opened up and made a Turner sandwich, squeezing him between us.

"Hey, I want some too," Stacia said as she joined us. It felt nice, really nice.

My mom said *The Breakfast Club* movie was about a group of unique teenagers forced together who discover they have a lot more in common than they thought. Thinking of my friends, there may be something to that. I couldn't imagine them not being in my life now.

After breakfast, we were back in our room, talking about last night. It was a lot to process. Turner cleared his throat, hesitated and asked, "What about the symbol? We haven't talked about it, but..."

The others looked to me. But it was Carrie, always the direct one, who asked, "This is your area, ghost girl, what does it mean?"

I shrugged. "I honestly don't understand it. Whoever—or whatever—wants to convey a message." For a while now.

Turner read my unspoken thought. "But you've seen this symbol for a while, right? It hasn't been just in the Crabtree firetrap." He looked at me, his eyes conveying his warmth.

I nodded.

Stacia perked up. "I saw it before, too. It was like someone had drawn the symbol with a finger on Abbey's sheet. And you said you watched it being drawn onto the wall of Charlotte's classroom."

"Yeah, that was the first I'd seen of it."

"Peas," Turner added, "it was on your plate of peas."

"Peas?" Carrie asked. "Really?"

I smiled. "My father always told me not to play with my food. So I'm at dinner the other week, and I look down to see a ghost had been playing with my food. It would have been funny if the circumstances hadn't been so scary."

"It was a little funny," Turner said with a grin. "If someone's trying to get your attention, it certainly worked."

"It's not as if the other times were hard to miss," I blurted.

"Others?"

Looking down, I suddenly found my toes to be especially fascinating.

"Others?"

"Well, there have been a few. On the bathroom mirrors, backstage at the theater and on the windows—every window actually —of Crabtree Hall."

"Really? Why didn't we see those?"

"I would guess they weren't meant for you." I'm the ghost girl, remember?

Carrie was on her feet, pacing the small space. "Let me work this out. We each saw the symbol during our escape from Crabtree Hall. We were meant to see them because we needed to find the symbols to escape. Someone wanted us to survive what most certainly would be a deathtrap. That makes sense. But Abbey, you started seeing the symbol before our rescue. Someone wants you..." Her words trailed off. The room fell silent as Carrie continued her pacing. "Someone wants you to..."

Carrie paused her pacing, and knelt in front of me, taking my hand. Looking into my eyes, she offered, "Abbey, whatever the symbol represents, it means something for you. And only you. This feels personal, not like some random spirit from the other side is here messing with you. Somewhere, possibly deep in your memories, the symbol is there. And when it comes to you, everything will make sense. I love you, ghost girl, and I know you'll figure this out."

I just hoped it would happen soon.

32

LATE NIGHT DOODLING

It was 2 a.m. and I couldn't sleep.

My mind raced without respite, as recent events played out repeatedly in my head. If that wasn't enough, the startlingly vivid images, sounds and emotions from the symbol's glowing transference revisited me. As before, it was too much to process. I closed my eyes for a long moment, as I began to control my body, slowing my breathing, slowing my mind, gaining control. Meditating on those strange thoughts, I was then able to examine them.

Faces, someone running, emotions, different languages. I couldn't understand what was being said, couldn't recognize the language, but I knew the joy that was expressed suddenly turned into fear. Shouts —that felt more like commands—echoed in my mind. The images of foreign looking faces and exotic locales were familiar, even though I was certain it wasn't anywhere I'd visited.

Focusing my breathing, I was able to slow the images down even further, replaying it like a film from the beginning. This time, I consciously examined every frame searching for the symbol. Because these strange thoughts sprung from touching the symbol, it would make sense the meaning behind it would be revealed to me. However, sense didn't appear to have a part in this—the symbol wasn't there.

When my mom first played, "I Still Haven't Found What I'm Looking For" for me, she said U2 spoke about her generation's need for deeper fulfillment and their futile search. Though I hadn't really gotten it then, I was finally beginning to understand what she meant. I knew a thing or two about futile searches.

FRUSTRATED, I sat up. The clock glowed 3:13. Clearly, sleep wasn't going to be an option tonight. Ms. Neuman said when you couldn't sleep and your mind was racing, you needed to remove things, not add them. She said writing out your thoughts was the best way to remove things, while reading and watching TV usually made things worse as they added things.

Flipping on my reading light, I opened a notebook to a blank page. My pen sat on the first line, poised for action. However, the words didn't cooperate. Unsure how to begin, I started doodling subconsciously. My pen leisurely drew an elegant looping line down and across the page. Lifting the pen, I brought it three quarters of the way back up and let the point rest on the paper. Almost by itself, the pen moved horizontally across my original line leaving behind a shorter wavy one. Lifting the pen, I brought it to rest just to the right of my vertical line. The pen sat there, waiting. Waiting.

It was at this moment I become aware of what my doodle had become.

I shouldn't be at all surprised. What else had I been dwelling on forever? And I didn't feel as if I'd made any progress whatsoever. Out of anger, I threw the notebook across the room, watching it hit the wall and slide to the floor—the symbol face up, mocking me.

Ugh, I just wanted to scream. It looked like Ms. Neuman was wrong this time. This hasn't help me fall sleep. Just the opposite.

All hope of sleep abandoned, I grabbed the CIA's Guidebook to Venezuela and sat on the floor leaning against my bed. Starting from the back, I flipped through the pages, not really reading the words. My mind was moving too fast to read. The images of Venezuela popped out at me as I sped through the book, page-by-page, chapter-by-chapter. Moving so fast, I more absorbed the pictures than studying them.

The feeling came roughly three quarters of the way through: I'd been here before—which was crazy, because I hadn't. In all the travels with my father, we've never been to South America. I suspected he purposely avoided taking assignments bringing us anywhere that reminded him of my mother's disappearance. Not that she was ever very far from my thoughts—or likely his as well. The question remained: why did it feel so familiar?

I continued my rapid pace through the book, flipping through each page like a high school boy's first *Playboy* magazine. This blistering pace continued until I reached the executive summary at the front of the book. The section was laid out by geographic region, featuring a satellite image with an overlaid map detailing each area, along with highlights of the specific region.

My finger had paused resting on a map. I recognized the region as the ultra-violent area near the Colombia border—the area with the mass amphibian kill that so freaked out Stacia and me earlier. Another coincidence? My finger traced along a river, thinking about all those dead frogs killed by the drug chemicals dumped into the river. 50-gallon drums of poison poured out up there, killing everything along the way, as the chemicals made their way down to there. The drugs were bad enough, with most destined for the US, via Colombia's cartels, but to ruin the environment for years to come with no regard for the native Venezuelan people...well, that was just wrong.

As my finger traced along the river's path, I stopped. And screamed.

33

THE RETURN OF
BRIAN A. THOMPSON,
ATTORNEY-AT-LAW

S tacia was out of bed, frantically scanning our room for the threat. Her wide eyes looked for the source of the screams. There weren't any scary clowns or knife-wielding homicidal maniacs. No ghostly figures with hands wrapped around my throat, squeezing the life from my body. Just Abbey, the ghost girl from Woodbury, Minnesota.

"Oh my God, Stacia. I know."

"Know what, Abbey? What is it?" Her confusion apparent, her concern obvious.

"I need to talk to my dad. Right now." I lunged for the bedside table, looking for my cell phone. Speed dial #2 got my father's phone ringing. As before, it frustratingly went to voicemail.

"Dad, I need you right now. Please call the second you get this. It's a matter of life or...well, a matter of life." A recorded voice came on, telling me my father's voicemail was full and my message wasn't retained. *Son of a...* I slammed the phone down.

Now what? Who could I tell? No adult was ever going to believe me. My eyes held Stacia's, her concern turning into worry. "Abbey?"

"Who's going to help me, Stacia?"

"I'm here," she offered in a tentative voice. No doubt believing her roommate had gone far, far off the deep end.

"I'm here...to help," I echoed. Yes! Frantically scrolling through my call list, I found his number and hit the call button.

"Abbey, it's 4:30 in the morning. Who are you calling?"

"Brian Thompson, attorney at law, of course. He can help. He has to."

The voice on the other end was thick with sleep, but still recognizable. "Brian Thompson, Attorney-at-Law. I'm here to help."

Thank God.

Not many adults would even listen—let alone believe—a frantic 14-year-old girl at 4:30 in the morning. Yet, at 7 a.m. sharp, Brian Thompson, attorney at law, was at my door.

"Hello, Miss Hill," he began. I grabbed his collar and pulled him into our room. Patience was not my strong suit this particular morning.

Rapidly telling the story, I held nothing back. Other than an occasional raised eyebrow, my attorney, Brian Thompson, appeared to believe me—which was strange, as I barely believed it myself. However, deep down I knew it was true. Every word. There was absolutely no other explanation.

My attorney was very professional, taking notes—on a legal pad I presumed—and asked clarifying questions as he drew more information out of me. Stacia was quiet the entire time, nodding her affirmation as the Crabtree Hall events unfolded. When his questions appeared to be entirely answered, Brian Thompson set down the pad and leaned forward.

"Before I was an attorney, I had another life. I was in naval intelligence for twenty years. When you spend that much time working in intelligence, you get to know a lot of people in similar capacities within our government. In those circles, as well as in adult life, favors are traded to help each other meet their objectives. Lucky for you, Miss Hill, I made way more deposits into the favor bank than withdrawals."

On his feet, Mr. Thompson said, "No promises, but I'll make some calls. It's an hour later in Washington, so I should be able to reach someone—though these types of people don't tend to sleep much. I'll be in touch," he said, shaking my hand and headed out with my book under his arm.

You come and go, you come and go. I can picture Boy George singing "Karma Chameleon" as I pondered the twist life had thrown my way. Eighties music had always framed how I processed things and this morning was no different. This music brought me joy and gave me a positive attitude and hope for the future. I glanced down at my folded hands and prayed the future will bring me joy—among other things.

34

SAYING OUR GOODBYES

The morning sun shone through my window, introducing me to my last day of Camp ToughLove. Adrenaline propelled me from my bed; no lingering for this girl. This was going to be a big day.

"Wake up, Stacia," I said giving her a shake. "Today's the day. Last day here."

The adrenaline hit her too and she rolled right out of bed, landing awkwardly on the floor looking much like a hot dog rolled into a crescent roll. We were both laughing as she struggled out of her blanket prison. "Hey, it's not easy being me you know," she said with playful exasperation. "You try it for a day."

"No thanks, there's already too many of you." She shot me one of her looks. I knew when I got that look, I'd scored a point with her. Stacia was all about the witty repartee. My banter had significantly improved after spending the summer together. To tell the truth, I was confident my life would never be the same.

The funny thing was, I always thought my life was okay. My dad and I learned to cope—and thrive actually—after my mom's disappearance. Life changed, we adapted, and I became good at some things, got really good at avoiding other things and life just kept living. Smooth and steady. But let in some friends, allow yourself to share fears and feelings and you begin to grow.

And then there was the physical aspect. You never know what you're capable of until you push yourself, competing with others— and yourself. I've gained tremendous strength and confidence from the challenges I've faced. I wouldn't recommend anyone risk their life the way I have, but it does have profound aftereffects. Your perspective changes; it has to. When you realize what's important—and I mean the really *important* things in your life—you have to think differently. The quest to fit in, popularity, what to wear or not wear, the near constant worry about what others will think about you...well, it just wasn't so important anymore.

THE END of camp came with not so much a bang—been there, done that—but a whimper. Mr. Kindle and the rest of the camp leadership addressed us outside the University Center. We were fidgeting on the hard metal folding chairs facing the front steps as Mr. Kindle spoke.

"Camp ToughLove is about love. Most of you have had difficult lives, faced difficult choices, and unfortunately had difficult results. Because someone loved you—or maybe it was a court appointed representative—a choice was made that brought you here.

"Camp ToughLove is about personal responsibility. In life, we are the ones responsible for each choice we make. It's not other people or events that are responsible for the way we think and feel. It is your life, and you are in charge of it.

"Camp ToughLove is about strength. As our Ms. Neuman likes to say, there will always be falling cows. Life isn't always going to be smooth and predictable. She tells the story of a family driving underneath a cliff and a 600-pound cow dropped onto their new car. A foot or so over and they would have been dead. In your life, kids, cows will drop. You won't see them coming, and you won't know what happened until it's over. The only thing you can do is accept it and roll with whatever life throws your way. Hopefully, we've made you physically and mentally strong enough to deal with life's difficult circumstances. It's how you react to adversity that makes you who you are. Becoming a whiner, saying that life isn't fair—or worse, running to your overprotective parents—will get you nowhere. Remember, it's your life. Take charge and deal with it."

Mr. Kindle paused, looking around the group, attempting to

make eye contact with each of us. This went on for a very long half minute.

"Camp ToughLove is about working with each other. Many of you are here because of your inability to relate to others. Let me tell you, being an angry loner is not all it's cracked up to be. You need other people. It's that simple. God put you here on this planet to be with other people. And I don't mean simply co-existing with each other—our relationships matter. I've learned people will forget what you said, people will forget what you did, but people will never forget how you made them feel. Be a blessing to others and your life will be immeasurably richer."

I looked over my shoulder. There were quite a few parents and families listening and waiting. Scanning the new arrivals, I searched for my father. He was nowhere in sight.

"We want to thank you for giving us your summer." The staff fanned out across the landing, all holding hands and Mr. Kindle continued. "We realize it may not have been your choice to be here, however, this could be the summer that changes your life forever. All we ask is you allow yourself to be changed. With that, Ms. Neuman will offer our closing prayer."

Changing places with Mr. Kindle, Ms. Neuman leaned into the microphone. "Please close your eyes and bow your heads." After a brief pause, she continued, "Heavenly Father, we want to thank you for each and every soul here. Be with each of your children as they go back out into the world. Wrap them up in your loving arms and help them to realize they are not alone in this world. Help them to find others to lean on, as well as others who need their newfound strength. We ask that each child of God here will go out and become a light for you, taking whatever life throws at them, and let them shine magnificently just as coal becomes diamond under the highest heat and the heaviest imaginable pressure. Bless each child, giving them purpose, filling them with your strength, your hope, and your love, allowing them to become the change our world so desperately needs. In your Son's name, Amen."

Mr. Kindle's next words were the most welcome words of my summer: "You are dismissed. See you next year."

A cheer rang out through the University Plaza and welcome chaos reigned. Families swarmed, hugs happened and tears flowed. I made my way through the crowd, unable to locate my habitually late father. When he dropped me off, he said he would be here, promising his assignment would be completed in time. I hoped he was correct.

"Abbey," I heard my name. It was Carrie with a big hug and a bigger smile. "These are my parents and this is my big sister, Jenna." A pleasant looking family stood behind Carrie, offering warm smiles.

"Nice to meet you all," I said. "I wouldn't be here now if it wasn't for Carrie pushing me the entire summer." Wrapping her up, I gave her a big squeeze.

"That's Carrie," said her sister, Jenna. "She's always going to push you."

"I love this girl," I said. "She can push me anytime."

"You have my number, so stay in touch," Carrie said. I was going to miss her.

STACIA FOUND me with a squeal and a lunging tackle-like hug. "I am not saying goodbye," she said with a tear. Her emotions thickened her voice. "I will see you this weekend. You are, and forever will be, my new sister."

"Truly," I said with a wink.

"Oh no," the blonde woman behind her said. "You didn't bring out your fake French sister, did you? Oh, Stacia. What am I going to do with you?"

"I made her a southern belle this time, the accent was a lot more fun to do."

I laughed as Stacia scooped up her little sister. The dark haired girl gave a joyous shriek. "I love Truly! She's funny." This made us all laugh and it felt very, very nice.

WALKING THROUGH THE THINNING CROWD, I was still a fatherless orphan. But, I knew he would come. There was someone else I searched for as I made my way through the happily reunited crowds. From the look on Turner's face, he'd been searching for me as well.

"Abbey," he said with a nervous formality, "I would like you to meet my father, William Dalton." A stern-faced man with a military-style haircut stepped forward thrusting a calloused hand into mine.

"It is a pleasure to meet you, Miss Hill. My son has been telling me about the challenges your group faced together. By all accounts, it was a harrowing experience. Turner said you played a significant part in the successful outcome. Thank you."

"Sir, I can honestly say without your son's ingenuity and support, I would not be standing here today. I've never seen anyone who can improvise and think on their feet as quickly as your son. You should be proud of the man he has become." I held his gaze, using the strength of my will to get him to acknowledge Turner's contribution. It seemed to work.

Mr. Dalton stepped next to his son, putting an arm around Turner. It took a long moment, but he looked at Turner, "I know I don't say this enough, but I am proud of you, son."

"Thanks, Father," Turner said. "Could I get a minute with Abbey to say goodbye?"

"I'll give you two," Mr. Dalton said with a trace of a smile.

Turner took my hand and pulled me to a bench. Still holding my hand, he looked into my eyes. "Abbey, I'm not sure what to say. I just don't want it to be goodbye."

"Turner, maybe we should stay friends. You are someone I can talk to, someone I trust with my feelings. And I haven't had anyone like that for years." It tore me up inside to say this.

Turner shook his head. His eyes held mine. "Love is friendship set on fire, Abbey. It's everything that friendship offers and more. You won't lose our closeness or your safety net. Love takes all we have and makes it deeper, fuller, and more alive. I used to sleep a lot, but not anymore. For once in my life, my reality is better than my dreams. You have to be the most amazing girl I've ever met and I don't want to lose you."

Wow. He was really good at this. I was sweating, and yet I had goosebumps. It sounded like the flu, but more likely, it was my turbocharged hormones. I touched a trembling hand to Turner's cheek. "Let's stay in touch and see what happens. I do love you, Turner Dalton."

I don't know how it came to happen, Turner leaned in and...it was amazing. His soft tender lips were on mine and I was transported to a warm, wonderful place. A place where I could get totally lost. Not surprisingly, another Eighties classic popped into my head. "Sweet Dreams (Are Made of This)." I'd dreamed of this moment, like absolutely for ever, and I didn't want it to end.

But it did, with a single word.

"Abbey?" It was my father.

35

WHAT KIND OF
CHURCH CAMP IS THIS?

"Daddy?"

Trying to re-engage my brain, I looked up to find a most welcome sight. "Daddy!" I screamed and wrapped him up in a bear hug, which he returned with equal passion. I was crying as all the emotions of the last six weeks flooded out like a broken fire hydrant.

"Sweetheart, I missed you too. I wish I could have called, however, the arrangement mandated no calls out. My cell was confiscated on day one and I still haven't gotten it back. Funny story," my dad said with a smile, "apparently the duty sergeant who took it had the worst case of diarrhea—"

"Wait, Dad. Didn't you hear my messages? You have no idea what happened?"

My father looked perplexed. "Umm, no. Anything important?"

I glanced over at Turner, who was turning tomato red trying to hold in his laughter. His coughing fit was enough to set me off and I burst out laughing. Wiping away tears, I tried to regain my composure. However, one glance at my father's confused face got me laughing again. We were drawing a crowd as Renata, Corey, Amanda, Brooke, Ms. Neuman and Charlotte surrounded us. For once, it didn't bother me to be the center of attention. I was relieved to see Stacia and Carrie squeeze their way through to join us.

Leave it to Stacia. Stepping up to my father and throwing her arms around him, Stacia shrieked, "Daddy!" The look on his face was priceless, as his outstretched arms didn't seem to know what to do. Eventually, one hand gently patted her on the back. Too funny.

Carrie slid an arm around me, "Hey there."

"That's my dad," I proudly told her.

"I guessed that," Carrie said with a grin.

"Dad, these are my friends, Carrie and Turner. I see you've already met Stacia," I said with a smile.

Looking as perplexed as having three Qs and trying to figure his next word in one of our Scrabble games, my father asked, "So what went on here? It must have been exciting."

Turner stepped up. "I've got this one. We were assigned into groups for a scavenger hunt and our group—me, Stacia, Carrie and Abbey—ended up in a deserted building by mistake. The building was struck by lightning, starting the entire building on fire leaving us trapped in the basement. The fire inspector later told us the lightning hit the top floor, but the current surged through the cabling and blew out the electrical system in the basement causing an explosion and fire. Your daughter was able to lead us through the maze of fires, blocked hallways, and collapsed floors. And she found the needle-in-a-haystack tunnel out of the building, just as the whole thing was collapsing on top of us. Simply amazing."

Another of my favorite songs from the Eighties was "Der Kommissar." Rather than the song, it's the group's name that pops into my Eighties-infused brain: After the Fire. Since the fire, I'd had time to reflect and give thanks for the special help I received. Giving my father a knowing smile, I said with a wink, "I may have had a little help, if you know what I mean."

Putting a weary hand to his forehead, he replied, "Oh, man. Yeah, I believe I know what you mean." He looked at Turner, Stacia and Carrie, who gave him solemn nods in return. The rest of the crowd didn't have a clue what actually happened in that building—and I wanted it to stay that way.

Quickly looking to change the subject, I happily added, "But everything ended well, right? We may not have won first place in the hunt, but we were given a special camp award for teamwork and overcoming adversity. And at a handy 8-1/2 by 11 size, I've been told it's suitable for framing."

Carrie jumped in, too. "All our military-style physical training actually paid off. There's no way we could have made it through the fiery deathtrap without it."

My father had regained his perplexed expression. "Military-style physical training? What kind of church camp is this?"

This time, I wasn't the only one laughing. It was pretty much the entire group, as most knew the story of my father's mistaken camp registration. "Umm, Dad," I started. That was until a honking Jeep sped around the curve and came to a rather abrupt stop at the curb. I recognized the driver. It was my attorney, Brian Thompson.

36

THE SHORT CHAPTER

"Hey, Miss Hill," Mr. Thompson shouted as he leaned through the open window. "Miss Hill!" He waved furiously and for good measure hit the horn again to catch my attention. It worked. He had my full attention.

"Who is that?" my father asked.

"He's my attorney," I said as I jogged down to the Jeep, completely unprepared for the shocking sight.

My wind was completely knocked out and both knees picked that moment to buckle. Mr. Thompson's quick reactions were the only thing that saved me from a less than graceful face plant into the door of his Jeep.

"Never Gonna Give You Up" is as iconic as any Eighties song can be. Most everyone seemed to know the song. Rick Astley's hit had my mom and I dancing many a day in our kitchen. Even though she's been gone, I was never going to give her up. And it was a good thing.

My mind was racing, yet I had no possible idea what to say at a moment like this.

Fortunately, my mom did. "Hi, Abbey."

37

Sometimes it's Really Good

Sitting on the other side of my attorney was my mother. Looking at me with her incredibly bright eyes was a very much alive Dr. Katherine Hill. Ever since I told Mr. Thompson the symbol's meaning, I'd hoped and prayed she was alive. After seeing the ghostly symbol repeatedly, and finding it matched up perfectly to the river in western Venezuela, I knew she was alive. The sense of urgency I felt wouldn't have been there otherwise.

I wanted to go to her, but I was rooted in place as Mr. Thompson spoke. "You were right, Abbey," he said. "The spot on the map next to the river was the rebel guerrilla camp where your mother was being held. They were using her as their own private physician. A special ops team was able to put together an operation to get to her and airlift her out. Believe it or not, the hardest part was getting someone to believe a small-town Wisconsin attorney having credible intelligence about Colombian guerrillas operating inside Venezuelan borders. But like I said earlier, some important people owed me favors."

"Abbey?" My father asked as he approached us.

"Daddy, I found Mom. She was..."

"Constantine!" My mother ran around the end of the Jeep toward my father.

"Katherine?" The complete range of possible emotions surged across my father's face and settled in on relief, pure sweet relief. And he grabbed my mother and simply held on, holding her like he'd never let go of her again. It was absolutely beautiful.

I gave them their moment and then joined in. My daddy was crying, my mom was sobbing and I completely lost it.

Looking into my mom's face, there were new lines, the last several years obviously having been hard ones. But it was the most welcome face in this entire world.

"Thank you so much, Abbey," she said touching my cheek. "Brian told me everything on the way over here. I know you hate what you have, and you think it's a curse. I'm here to tell you, it's not. You have a gift, Abbey. A wonderful gift."

Wiping away my tears, I nodded. "I know that, Mom. It's part of me. It saved our lives here this summer." I gestured to my friends. "Without it, none of us would be here."

My attorney, Brian Thompson, stepped up to us. I surprised him with a hug, my feet off the ground. "Thank you so much. I don't know what I would have done without you. You are the best attorney in the entire world. I don't think I could ever repay you."

"Well, there is the matter of my bill," he said with an envelope appearing in his hand, an unreadable expression on his face.

"We've got that," Ms. Neuman said, stepping forward as she took the envelope. "It's the least we could do for you, Abbey."

"Thank you, but it's not necessary," I told her. "If there was one thing worth paying for, it's Mr. Thompson's legal fees."

"It's only a dollar?" Ms. Neuman said, with the opened envelope in hand, confusion on her face.

"Only a dollar," my attorney, Brian Thompson said with a grin. "Miss Hill qualified for my student discount. I have payment plans available, as well. Though, your credit will always be good with me."

I frickin' love this guy.

"You know, I have a strange idea," I said to the group. An idea, like a ghost, must be spoken to a little before it will explain itself. "Despite almost dying in the middle of our scavenger hunt, despite the grueling physical training, the possessed soccer players and even the field of squishy dead frogs, I will miss this place." As I looked around at my new friends, I finally began to understand why.

John Cougar Mellencamp's Eighties song, "Hurts So Good," told our story. Sure, camp was tough. We had pain and suffering, trials and tribulations, but it brought us together. It made us better and I'd changed. The experience had given me newfound strength and confidence.

Maybe my idea wasn't so strange after all.

My father looked around, a goofy smile on his face—the weight of the world now completely lifted from his shoulders. "This certainly is an odd church camp, isn't it?"

Laughing, I wrapped my arms around my parents, squeezing them tight. "You have no idea."

Sometimes it was really good to be the ghost girl.

38
THE FUTURE'S SO BRIGHT

"Hey, Mom, you know what I'd really like to hear?" I asked as I pulled out the mixer.

"Let me guess. Some Britney or Beyoncé? Maybe some Garth or Dolly?" She set the chocolate chips next to the flour and sugar on the counter and headed for the refrigerator.

"Umm, no," I replied. Baking cookies was always a special time at our house. A time for my mom and me to unwind, spend time together, spill some flour and rock out to Eighties music.

Returning with several sticks of butter, my mom gave me a pretend perplexed look. "How about rap or opera?"

"Mom."

"Wait," she said with a grin, "I think it's coming back to me. Who can forget those awesome band names: Simply Red, Dream Academy, Timbuk 3, Escape Club, INXS, Squeeze, and one of my favorites, Kajagoogoo."

"Yes," I said, pumping my fist into the air. "I'm happy the experience wasn't so traumatic you'd forgotten about our favorite music. It helped me through the tough times."

My mom came over and hugged me. "Sweetie, it helped me too. There's something about music that strengthens, offers hope, and transports you back to happier times. It's a powerful thing. And if that isn't the definition of coping, I don't know what is."

"Was it difficult being there?" I held her eyes looking for some sign of the hardship she must have endured.

Brushing back my hair, my mom shook her head. "At first I was terrified. They'd grabbed me from a market and put a cloth bag over my head."

"I can imagine how terrifying that would be," thinking back to the day when I experienced something similar at camp.

"I was thrown into the back of a truck and we bounced along on what had to be the worst road in all of South America—if it was even a road at all. Eventually, they pulled the hood off when I told them I'd never be able to identify where we were anyway. When you've seen one jungle, you've seen every jungle."

We both leaned against the counter, our chocolate chip cookie baking forgotten for the moment.

"Why did they take you?"

"They just needed a doctor. I was taken to a drug processing facility near the Colombian border where they had a large chemical spill. Workers had gotten sick and needed treatment."

Nodding, I said, "I hear that happens down there."

"More often than it should. They're more than careless with something so toxic. And I told them so."

"How did they take that?" Though the last thing I wanted to hear was people being mean to my mother.

"Surprisingly, pretty well. But, by then I'd built up credibility with treating patients and establishing a mini clinic. I made them see how they were hurting their profits and exposing themselves to international discovery by being so reckless with chemicals. Unfortunately, I made myself a little *too* valuable and they didn't want to let me go. I'm so happy you figured out where I was."

She reached over and wiped away my tears.

"It was a multigenerational effort," I told her. "I'm convinced it was Grandma leading me out of the burning building. It took me a while to figure it out, but she showed me where you were, too. She'd been trying to send me a message for a while. It had to be Grandma."

She laughed and said, "That doesn't surprise me at all, she always looked out for us. I'm also pretty confident she's passed her gift onto you."

I nodded, knowing she was right. "I'm just happy you're home."

Dumping the sugar and butter in the mixer bowl, I asked mom for the vanilla as I cracked the eggs. After she poured the teaspoon into the bowl, I said, "I know it wasn't easy for you being held in the jungle, but it was difficult for us, too. We didn't know what happened, where you were or if you were even alive. But I thought you were and I even talked to you sometimes."

I smiled, but a tear still found its way down my cheek. "It was hard, but eventually life went on. We had a sort of uneasy equilibrium here, both of us thinking about you, but neither talking about you. Guess we didn't want to get the other upset."

"Sweetie."

"We had each other though. I've gotten really good at being Dad's research assistant. Except for this last trip when I couldn't go. But the thing was, we were surviving." I paused as I was ready to ask the difficult question. "Are you going back there again? I know how much you love Venezuela, but I'm not sure I could take it if you left us again." I could feel my lip tremble as I asked.

Mom shook her head. "No honey, that ship has sailed. It's time I planted my roots here. In fact, I have an interview tomorrow to be an emergency room physician for the University hospital. Would you like that?"

I hugged her as tight as I could. I think it was answer enough.

My father joined us, peeking into the mixing bowl and looking over the pile of ingredients. "Hmmm, I like what I see here. If I'd known you were going to make cookies when you got back home, I would have suggested Abbey rescue you a lot earlier."

"Dad!" I exclaimed—and then promptly snorted with laughter.

That got us all laughing.

"I was wondering about the camp, Constantine," my mother said to my dad. "You signed her up for the wrong camp. Or did you?"

Shaking his head, my father said, "No, I really did. It was a mix up, plain and simple. The same organization ran both camps, both the church and the boot camps. I was moving too fast and missed the fact the church camp had ended. But it all worked out, didn't it?"

I thought of my new friends, Stacia and Carrie. And Turner. "I guess it did." I smiled. "How about that music, Mom?"

"Rogers and Hammerstein's greatest hits? Maybe some John Denver?" she asked as she went over to the music player.

"How about something we can dance to?" Dad asked.

"You're speaking my language. Eighties it is." And the sound of Bruce Springsteen singing "Dancing in the Dark" filled the kitchen. My father grabbed my mother's hand and they began to dance. She giggled as he lifted her hand to try to twirl her. I flipped off the overhead light and watched my goofy parents frolicking together, dancing in the dark of our kitchen once more.

Ah, life was good. And the future was so bright (I gotta wear shades).

ACKNOWLEDGMENTS

Anyone who has had a book published knows that without the many people who've added their assistance, inspiration, background, feedback and support, the book wouldn't have come to fruition. Abnormally Abbey is no different and I'd like to thank:

First and foremost, my wife, Jen Daly, for her love and support. Her ability to be a sounding board is near-legendary in my opinion. This book would not be in your hands without her.

My family: Abbey, Andrew, Cade, Ben, Dan and Suzanna, who patiently listened as I went on endlessly about story ideas.

Anastacia Smith for her inspiration for Abbey's friend, Stacia, as well as all the friends who inspired many of the book's characters. To paraphrase a common legal disclaimer: any resemblance to actual persons, living or dead, is meant to be a compliment.

Ian Punnett (@deaconpunnett) for his thoughts on the theology of ghosts. I enjoyed our conversation over warm cinnamon rolls and hot chocolate.

My beta reader, Kristin Yodock, Ph.D., for her great questions and suggestions.

The organizers of #PitMad that led to my publisher finding me. Twitter is a better place because of you.

Thanks to everyone on the Immortal Works team who helped me so much. Special thanks to my editor Mark W. Woodring, and Holli Anderson, Chief Editor, for getting my manuscript in such good shape, and Ashley Literski, for a great cover. A special thanks to Staci Olsen, Acquisitions Editor, for discovering me in the first place.

And lastly, to authors John Sandford and Stephen King. Your brilliant storytelling (demonstrated by the fact I could never put your books down) inspired me to begin writing in the first place.

ABOUT THE AUTHOR

Allan Evans lives in the Twin Cities of Minnesota with his blended family and three unruly dogs. An advertising copywriter by day and a writer of fiction by night, he enjoys telling a good story. A youth soccer coach, you can usually find him on a soccer field somewhere.

This has been an
Immortal Production